Christmas at the Shore

Angela Lewis Buckner

DEDICATION

To My Momma

Thank you for giving me a love for all creative things and for living a life that has been a template to show me that anything is possible. Your zeal and excitement are the tools that push others forward to do great things. Watching you live your life has taught me more than a 1000 books could ever teach.

As you read the pages of this book, I hope you find yourself within and see how your love for art and for the beautiful sea have influenced my life.

I love you.

.

ACKNOWLEDGMENTS

To my children and husband, you are my world. Thank you for always supporting me and pushing me forward into the unknowns of this thing we call life. I would not be the person I am today without you all.

CHAPTER 1

I hadn't seen my father in a few weeks. I mean, we are close, but the busyness of life had gotten in the way of multiple visits. When mom first died, I tried to visit him every other day. We would take walks or look at old photos and talk about her and sometimes we would just sit on their front porch in silence. He still lived in the house that I grew up in and I suppose it would always be like home to me. It was located on one of the quietest, most beautiful streets of our town. Even though the town had grown over the years, this street remained pretty much the same. Lined with sidewalks and streetlights, it always had people passing by. Just ordinary people, mostly younger families that had inherited the homes from their parents that were now too old to live alone. They were now raising their own families on the very same street. Sometimes they would walk by with an aging parent that had known my parents for years and that would be just the invite my father needed to strike up a conversation with them.

Fall was starting to settle into our northern town and it was my favorite season of all. The street was lined with Maple trees on both sides and the leaves would soon turn from summer's green to Autumn's fiery reds and yellows. They were such pretty colors that no one even bothered to rake or blow them until they had all fallen off the limbs where they had shaded us through the summer. They formed a vibrant carpet across the lawns.

My father had called the day before to ask me to stop by and I noticed a tiredness in his voice that wasn't normally there. He missed my mother horribly, but he worked to keep himself busy. Their marriage had stood the test of time and I only hoped that I would be so lucky one day. He kept busy by tinkering around his garage and he met friends for breakfast each week. He loved to read, so he became involved in a book club one night a week. I am pretty sure that he didn't love this new life of his, but sometimes we have to move forward just to keep ourselves from dying right where we are. They were married 49 years, but grew up in this town as neighbors and friends even before that. She died after having a stroke and left my dad to find a way to live his life without her.

My father had always worked hard and never saw any reason to miss work. Unless it was a holiday, he would be at his accounting firm every day. He never saw a doctor for anything, not even a check-up. The only exceptions to working all the time were our summer trips to the seashore. We had not been as a family since my last year of college. My parents loved the beach, especially my mother. She would take walks and read books and gather shells. She always seemed to have a seashell in a jacket pocket that she would find months after summer had passed. She loved it so much that my dad bought her a beach house in this little small town on the coast, but it had long since turned into a rental. The last time we visited the shore, my brother had gotten married, but now he was building a business and my sister's husband had just gotten relocated a couple hours further north. It was just too hard to find a time to visit. Then when mom had gotten sick, we never went back.

They had come home for mom's funeral, but left a few days later, leaving me and dad on our own. We were a close family growing up, living in a small town, but as we all grew older our lives went in different directions. I realized more and more that she was the glue that held us together and now that she was gone, we just didn't make visits a priority. Maybe it was just too hard. Now we only saw each other maybe once a year, if that.

Dad had always hoped my brother would take over his firm, so when he decided to go out and start his own agency in another town, he and dad had butted heads quite often and now they hardly knew how to talk to each other. My sister and I talked every couple of weeks, but she was busy with her life and I wasn't even married or engaged... or dating. So it looked like I would be the one to take care of dad, and take over his business. I had dreamed of someday having my own small Interior design shop, but felt like I needed to help my parents in their business. I loved taking old things and houses and imagining the new life they could have. I was always scanning the antique stores for that discarded perfect piece that I could breathe life back in to. Somehow it brought me peace that nothing else did. I got it from my mother. She loved to buy old things and give them a new life. Somedays, I could hear her voice in my head. She always encouraged me to follow my own dreams. And sometimes I saw the smallest reminders that she was still with me.

CHAPTER 2

I pulled down the street and noticed the leaves were already starting to color on the tips. I made a mental note to come over and see them in a week or so. I pulled in the driveway and dad was on the front porch waiting for me with a glass of sweet tea. I kissed him on the cheek and sat down. He looked more tired than he had sounded the phone.

"Are you alright dad, you sounded tired on the phone," I asked.

He said, "Well to be honest, I'm not sure. I have been so tired lately and it seems that I have to have a nap or two everyday just to make it."

"Have you been going out more or going for longer walks?"

"No," he said, "I haven't been able to go on a walk for weeks. I have been to the office a few times, but then I'm worn out.

"I think I may need a check-up or whatever those doctors call it. Just to be sure I'm running ok," he said nervously.

"Ok, dad, I will call and make an appointment with Dr. Bradley tomorrow, but don't worry, I'm sure you're fine. Maybe you just need some vitamins or to exercise more."

Dad was quieter than usual, but I spent the rest of the afternoon with him talking about the neighbors and who had remodeled their parent's homes and who had ended up selling their house to a brand new neighbor. I fixed us both some dinner, meatloaf with mashed potatoes. Dad loved mom's meatloaf, so I tried to fix it for him whenever I had the chance. He could cook as good as me, probably better, but he had resorted to microwave dinners over the last several years. Just easier I suppose. He still tried to work at the firm some, but had pretty much stepped back to let me run things.

I left him in his chair falling asleep watching an old movie. I tried not to worry much, but it was very strange to even be calling a doctor for my father. Maybe I should call and let my brother and sister know he wasn't feeling well. I drifted off to sleep deciding to wait until after his appointment. I'm sure it's nothing, no reason to worry them, but after mom's death, I couldn't help but worry a little myself.

CHAPTER 3

Dr. Bradley was able to see Dad on Thursday and he insisted on going alone. Of course, what father wants his daughter to tag along to a check-up at his doctor's office? My dad was one of the most independent men I had ever met and he sure wasn't about to let me go with him to this.

Dr. Bradley had been our family doctor since I was a kid. He had seen us through chicken pox, 3 times, a couple of broken arms, and more sore throats and colds than anyone could count. He was also Mom's doctor and had been a friend forever. We went to school with his kids and I think my sister may have even been the homecoming date to one of his sons. They were both doctors now and were working to take over his practice when he retired. I called Dad that evening to see how the appointment went. He said Dr. Bradley did some tests and wanted to do more and would see him back in two weeks. He told me not to worry, but I was starting to worry. Tests? What tests?

I made dad let me go back to see Dr. Bradley with him after the two weeks was over. They had taken blood work and done all sorts of scans. I had only visited my dad at his house, but now we were going out and I realized he was moving slower than I had ever seen him move. He acted like everything hurt. To put on his shoes, walk down the steps, getting in the car, getting out of the car. His face showed obvious pain that I hadn't noticed before.

"Are you alright, Dad?"

"You seem like you're hurting."

"I'm fine, Sammy, just moving a little slow these days."

My dad had called me Sammy for as long as I can remember. Everyone called me Sammy, but my dad started it when I was a baby. My given name was Samantha, but he had given us all nicknames that had stuck with us and in a small town, it truly *stuck* with us. My sister Elizabeth was Lizzy and my brother Michael was always called Mac. Even our teachers that knew our real names called us by these "given" nicknames.

The doctor's office was quiet and only had a few patients waiting when we got there. I signed dad in on the list and we sat down.

"You know it's silly that you took off work to drive me to this doctor's appointment," Dad said.

My dad never wanted anyone doting over him so this was new territory for both of us. The wait seemed to last forever, but finally the nurse called his name and took us to Dr. Bradley's office. I felt nervous and I could tell that dad wasn't so sure of himself either.

"Well hello, Sammy!" he said, "It's so good to see you again."

"Thank you, it's good to see you too."

"Well, John, we got all your tests results back and we need to discuss a few things. Your tests look ok, but not great, your blood pressure is high and you have put on a good bit of weight. It's time to make some major changes. You work too much and are too stressed, and I think it is causing your arthritis to flare up and make you hurt all over.

He looked at me, "Sammy, you still planning to take over the business?"

"Yes sir, that's the plan!" I said.

"Well, it's time to make it happen before your father here works himself into the grave."

"Hogwash, I'm fine. Just getting a little slow and achy in my old age!" Dad tried to resist, but Dr. Bradley was insistent.

"John, we've been friends for as long as I can remember and I'm telling you, it's time to take a long vacation and let Sammy step up into your shoes. She is well able."

"Okay, okay" my dad finally conceded, but not happily. "We will work something out and I will try to slow down."

Dr. Bradley continued to tell us that dad could suffer from a heart attack or stroke if he didn't make some changes soon. The stress was just too much for him.

So, my new mission….to get the most stubborn man in the world to make healthy lifestyle changes. This should be great fun! Over the next few weeks, I tried recipes, and exercises and anything I could think of to get my dad to make some changes but that saying about teaching an old dog new tricks was sure true. How did my mom cook for him all those years, no salad, no veggies? For sure, a meat and potatoes kind of man. And getting him to turn anything loose at the office was impossible. He wanted his hand in every account and a final look in every file. He didn't work at the office much, but clearly he wasn't letting it go like I had thought. I had finally reached the end of my rope one afternoon and just burst into tears! I was not normally a crier, but I was so frustrated.

"Dad, I can't do this anymore! You're impossible! You won't follow doctor's orders. You won't slow down, you won't change your habits and you won't change your diet. I'm trying to do everything plus run your business. I don't know what you want me to do."

He stood there for a minute.

"There is something you can do for me Sammy", Dad said quietly and calmly, like he did when I was a kid and was super frustrated and when I was a teenager and my world was falling apart. He always had that way of calming me down.

"I want to go to the seashore for Christmas." He quietly said.

"What?" I didn't think I heard him correctly. We hadn't even mentioned the beach since mom's funeral. I didn't think I could go back there.

"But dad, you're sick and tired, and that's a pretty long trip. I'm not sure we can do that. We would have to close the office for longer than normal and all the employees, I don't know. Besides, we haven't been there in years. What brought all this on?"

"I want to go there for Christmas and you're going to take me," he said stubbornly. "And you're going to invite your brother and sister and we're going to have a nice Christmas!" And that was that.

I drove home thinking about how much my mother must love watching this from heaven. How she must smiling at the thought of me having to go back there.

CHAPTER 4

The seashore, as dad called it, was an 8 hour drive from our home. We spent every summer there when I was a kid. My parents loved the small town and every year they dreamed of having their own home there someday. Then one day, dad surprised my mom with the keys to that beach house. It wasn't fancy, but it was ours! It was just an old house that sat near the beach just outside of the small bayside town. It was a Cape Cod style with a big porch, hardwood floors and open rooms with views of the ocean. The first thing my mother did was hang a big porch swing on that porch and we all spent the summers there reading, talking, laughing, and entertaining the occasional guest. I loved it there. The beach was my solace, my comfort, the place that I felt completely peaceful. I never wanted to leave, but I did leave and had not been back.

I think I got that from my mother. She would spend hours just walking along the shore, looking for the perfect shell or treasure. Her skin would tan a leathery brown and her eyes were as blue as the ocean. She just loved being there. She would wake up early and I would find her drinking her coffee on that old swing, just watching the tide roll in. She never tired of cooking huge dinners and I think it was her life's dream to just sit and watch all of us laugh and enjoy ourselves. Somehow when we were there, the cares of life and work all faded to the sound of the waves, the wind and our laughter. She said it was like heaven to her.

Every year the whole family looked forward to spending our summers in that house. Somehow, even Dad managed to rearrange clients and partners so that he could be there for a few weeks in the summer. He would travel back and forth for work, but we stayed the entire summer. Time went slow on those summer days in that quiet little town. We would spend hours at the beach playing in the ocean until we were waterlogged, then we would lay on the warm sand and watch the tourists. Later in the day, we would usually take our bikes down the street to the ice cream shop and try to eat our ice cream before it dripped from the cone in the warm summer sun. My sister Lizzy was never very good at that. She somehow always managed to drip it down both arms every time.

We would arrive at the beach Memorial Day Weekend ahead of the crowds and open up the dusty house. The first couple of days were spent cleaning and freshening, making beds and dusting, sweeping and hosing down porches, but as soon as Mom was satisfied with the cleaning, we were free to go.

She had a special room in the house that overlooked the blue water. She was an artist. Not a famous artist or anything, although she was very talented, but she loved to paint and create and I loved to watch her. She had passed that love of art on to me. I was as happy hanging out in her art room as I was on the beach. She wanted to visit again the last year of her life, but we just never made it happen. The shore held many wonderful memories for my family and me, and a couple not so wonderful ones too.

How was I supposed to convince my brother and sister to drop everything, and pack up and celebrate Christmas at our old beach house? They hardly ever took time to call Dad, much less, take time to have an extended visit...at Christmas! My brother would have to put work on hold, pack up his wife and kids, and somehow bring their Christmas to the beach and my sister would have to make time for something else in her life. Yea, probably not going to happen, but if that would make Dad happy and make him take a break, then I had to try.

My plan was to convince my brother's sweet wife, Amy, first. If I could win her over, he would have to agree. Then we could gang up on my sister, like when we were kids. I called Amy but didn't get an answer. I just left a message to give me a call.

My brother actually met Amy one summer at the beach while her family was on vacation, so maybe a walk down memory lane would convince her to take her family there for Christmas. They met my brother's freshman year in college and realized that they were in school about an hour from each other. When vacation ended for Amy's family, they stayed in touch and when school started again in the fall, they picked up right where they left off. They seemed to be a perfect fit for each other. Amy was sweet, she loved dad, and she would help me...maybe!

Amy called me back the next morning. After the "hellos" and initial questions about the kids, she asked about dad. So I jumped right in.

"Well, since you asked", I said. "Dad, is really tired and the doctor has told him he must take a break, a vacation, time off... completely off.

So I have a question for you." I paused, "now don't answer too fast, just think about it and how great it will be, and so romantic and such a great thing for your kids!"

"What are you talking about Sammy? How does this involve romance or the kids?"

"Well, Amy, Dad wants the whole family to go to the beach again...together."

"Oh, well that's not so bad, that could be pretty fun actually if we can work it out and I can talk your brother into taking off work."

So then I dropped the worst part.

"Yea, so he wants to have the vacation at Christmas, celebrate Christmas at the beach house."

"CHRISTMAS?" she yelled, and Amy was not a yeller. "He wants to have Christmas there? He wants everyone to drop all the crazy holiday events and pack up and go to the beach for Christmas? I don't know how that could possible work, Sammy."

It was time for my speech.

"I know it's hard and I know you and Mac are so busy and the kids have stuff going on, but Dad is really not feeling well and he won't do what the doctor says and this is all he wants. Just think, you could show the girls where you and Mac met and where you went on all those dates that summer before college. Hey, I could even babysit and you two could go out and visit those places and maybe rekindle a little romance, you know, like a little trip down memory lane."

I was one breath short of begging when she said, "Hmmm, it does sound kind of fun. I have often thought of that little beach town. Ok, I will try to convince your brother, but you're going to owe me two nights of babysitting and the house better look like Christmas when we get there because my kids will not be happy without a tree!"

"Ok it's a deal! Work your magic on my stubborn brother." I said, relieved.

Wait, did I just agree to decorate the house for Christmas too? What on earth was I getting myself into? I had to plan a trip to the beach, with family and dad and now add in Christmas décor! I had my doubts.

Now on to my sister. Lizzy should honestly be talking everyone into having this vacation because she is a charmer. She can talk anyone into just about anything. Maybe because she is the baby of the family, but when we were kids and Mac and I really wanted to go somewhere and we knew the answer would be a no, we pulled out the big guns and sent Lizzy in to ask Mom and Dad. Her sweet voice and those big blue eyes. They never told her no. How was I supposed to talk the queen of persuasion into this crazy vacation? Maybe I should have gotten her on board first.

"Hey Lizzy, how's it goin?"

"Hey Sammy! What's up, haven't talked to you in weeks, everything okay?"

"Well, yea, everything is pretty good, I have been crazy busy, but I need a favor. Well, Dad kind of wants a favor."

"Dad?" she sounded concerned, "is he okay?"

"Well, he has been really tired lately and the doctor said he needs to rest, stop working so hard. Maybe take a vacation."

At that point, Lizzy busted out laughing, "Sammy, Dad never took a vacation, when we used to go on vacation, so that's not going to happen."

"Well, he has decided he wants to do just that." I said slowly.

After explaining about the whole trip, she was sure that she would never be able to come, or to get her husband to take any extra days off work. He worked all the time and she had confided in me many times that their marriage had suffered because of it. She said she would try her best and get back to me so all I could do was wait. It was already October. Dad would be wondering if they were coming, but maybe he wouldn't ask before they got back to me.

I was so worried about them coming, I hadn't even stopped to think about whether or not I wanted to go. I guess I didn't have much of a choice at this point. I was very busy at the office, but I could gladly leave it behind for a couple of weeks...or forever. I had not been back to the beach once since that summer before my senior year in college, I just couldn't go back there and face the things I had walked away from. So, I never went back. I had long since put that summer behind me, but thinking about going back there brought it all back. That was the summer I met Kyle Martin. His family lived in that small town and we ran into each other at the marina where I was taking sailing lessons the shortly after we arrived that summer. We spent every day together and thought we were in love. I wanted to stay there after the summer was over, but I did what I thought would help my parents and went back to school to finish my accounting degree. We didn't even try a long distance relationship, I just left, and he joined the military or something. I don't know what happened to him. I went to work for Dad and I barely came up for air. I don't think of that beach without him crossing my mind. Maybe that's why I never went back. The beach was about Kyle and everything we had. I almost never got over that and I sure didn't want to rip the bandage back off again. No thanks.

CHAPTER 5

Getting Dad to rest was a job in its self. He would either show up at the office at 8 am or I would go to his house and he would be outside trimming hedges or straightening the garage. He had worked fifty or sixty hours a week my entire life so I understood that he just couldn't sit around, but he was supposed to be resting.

My schedule consisted of work, arguing with my dad, and taking him to doctor appointments. A week had passed and I had not heard a word from Amy or Lizzy and I didn't want to have to call them back. I did contact the property management company and tell them we would be using the house in December. They assured me that everything was pretty much the same and that it would be ready for our arrival.

Our beach house was in a sleepy little town, with mostly locals only in the winter months and a few snow birds, so the property was not rented in the winter. The last time I was there, the town only had a couple of restaurants, one grocery store, a hardware store and an ice cream shop. I wasn't even sure what the people who lived there did for a living. It was a beautiful town, but very quaint, nothing like the big city that I lived in now. I lived in a condo on the other side of town, near my office. I slept there and that was about it, so I never bothered to fix it up or have anyone over and as much as I used to love decorating, I hadn't done much of that either. I actually didn't have a lot of friends to speak of. I guess I don't have any friends other than the people I work with, I wasn't very social. Occasionally, we would have a quick dinner after work, but usually I went home or went to visit dad.

Lizzy finally called two days later and confirmed that she would be there the week of Christmas, but her husband was not going to make it. I was surprised that she would leave and spend Christmas without him, but I was thankful she was willing to make the effort.

"Are you sure that he won't come Lizzy? He doesn't want to be away from you at Christmas!"

"No, Sammy, he's not coming. He's too busy for trips, Christmas and for me. It's fine though. I will be there."

I was glad she was coming, because I knew I couldn't do this alone, but I couldn't help but be sad for her. They were so happy when they got married and they were inseparable. After a few years, his real estate business took off and she didn't even have to work anymore, but he worked enough for four people. He was always on his phone, always having to work on some deal. I had become a workaholic like my dad but my sister had married one. Maybe she needed this time away to give herself a break from all that and maybe he would change his mind. I didn't want to see her spend Christmas without him.

When Amy called back, she was happy to say that she had somehow talked Mac into making the trip but they wouldn't arrive until Christmas Eve. I was hoping for sooner, but I would take what I could get. I honestly didn't think he would come at all and probably wouldn't have except for her talking him into it. He and Dad had not been close for years, but since my mother had passed, he had nearly stopped coming to visit. They had two girls, Sara, who was ten and Sally who was eight. He brought them to see my mom whenever they could and they loved their Pop and Gram. He and Amy would never stay at the house during their visits but they would let the girls spend the night. It wasn't that he didn't love and appreciate my dad, but they always ended up butting heads about the same subject and he didn't want the girls to be around that. I was hoping this trip might mend some broken fences too.

So it was set, Dad and I would go to the house the first week of December and everyone else would come the week of Christmas. I would have to work from the home office there, but business slowed a little around Christmas and hit hard in January. I had about four weeks to prepare my dad's house, the business, and get ready for Christmas. Not even possible, but I had to try. I wasn't even sure where to start, but I was headed to the beach and back to my past.

Being the control freak that I am, I spent the next week at work assigning different accounts to other employees and making sure they knew every single detail about the client and their business. I didn't love my job but I was good at it. Then the following two weeks I spent making sure our houses were ready to close up for almost a month, stopped the mail, and tried to finish my Christmas shopping, and Dad's Christmas shopping. I had never even helped mom get the house ready to leave to go on vacation. I was sure I had forgotten something important and that one or both of our houses would be flooded, robbed, or broken into before January. All the while, in the back of my mind, I felt the dread of going back there.

Mom always did the packing for these trips. Making sure we had every little thing we needed for cooking and cleaning. She made a list in early spring before school even got out and everything from sunscreen to band aids were on that list. I hardly cooked at home, how was I going to cook for Christmas, a full Christmas dinner? Maybe there was a restaurant that served it and we could all go out to eat. Doubtful. I would worry about that later. Surely they had a decent grocery store nearby by now. There was only one small store when we were young and my mother swore their prices were highway robbery, but you had no choice but to purchase from them.

Even though it was the beach, it would be cold and possibly snowy, so I tried to make sure that we both had the clothes we would need. I packed my normal "off work" clothes: sweats, leggings, running shoes, slouchy sweater and decided to add one pair of jeans and a nice sweater just in case I had to look nice for some reason. When I wasn't working, my long hair was in a sloppy bun and I hardly wore any makeup, so packing for me was pretty easy. I had no one to impress.

All the preparation seemed to make Dad even more tired but he was hanging in there and trying to help. He packed all of his clothes and personal items, made sure his house was straightened and did a few other things that I had listed for him to do. He seemed happy to be going back to the beach house again and I was feeling kind of happy myself, when I wasn't worrying about my list. I knew tomorrow would be a long day.

We headed out early and Dad slept part of the way and that gave me time to think about this trip and whether or not Kyle's family still lived there. Surely he had moved away. Deep inside, I wished my mom was there, this was her thing. She loved having us all around for Christmas, but to be able to do it at our beach house would've meant the world to her. We should have made it happen. We arrived in the little town of Pier City, off the upper North Carolina coast, around lunch time. I was surprised to see it busy and bustling in the off season, but it was decorated for Christmas and was just as beautiful as I remembered. It had changed some over the past eight years, but not a lot. There were a couple more stores and it looked like the grocery store had been enlarged and maybe a few more restaurants, but basically it was the same sweet little town that I remembered.

We stopped at the store to pick up some groceries first because the house would be completely empty. We would need everything to fill the cabinets, but for now coffee and toilet paper and something for breakfast were our main necessities. I opened the car door and the smell of the salt air came rushing at me. People say smells can trigger memories. The salty air wrapped around me like a soft blanket, bringing with it the comforts of this sweet town.

Dad wanted to see the house as soon as possible so he was rushing me to get there. The property management company had always kept us updated on any issues or if anything ever needed to be replaced, but for the most part it was just a simple old house on the beach full of our childhood memories and some grown up ones too. It was Mom's house, her heart and all the things she loved.

CHAPTER 6

We drove about a half mile out of the little town with the beach on one side of us and the small houses on the other side. Most were freshly painted with bright colors and pretty porches. It was winter, but the sun was shining into the car sharing its warmth and all the colorful houses made me miss the summer. The road made a sharp left and went directly alongside the beach, but now we were riding between the beach front houses and the ones that were across the street from the beach. There were no high rise buildings or sets of condos in the town, so nothing blocked the view of the water. It was so beautiful. I had long forgotten how I used to feel when we would arrive and see the ocean, but here it was like an old friend, waiting for my return. I felt it again, almost.

I could see our house ahead, but it wasn't like the pretty colorful houses. It was faded and sad. The screened porch that held my mother's swing and heart was torn and shabby. My heart sank as I looked at my dad's face.

"It looks so old," he said. "Your mother would have hated the way I have let it go downhill".

"Oh Dad, it's just a little worn. We will have it fixed up in no time at all! Maybe I can hire someone to come do some work on it next week. We can clean the porch, cut the bushes back and it will be great!"

But Dad was right, it did look old. It looked sad and forgotten. I wanted to apologize for leaving it alone after all the wonderful memories it had given to me. I wanted to make it look happy and alive again. He was right, my mother would have been heartbroken to see it this way. I had to get it back for her as much as I could and for myself too. I would figure out a way to bring some life back into our beach house even if it was just long enough to say goodbye.

We parked on the driveway because it didn't have a garage. The brick was inlaid into the sand by my dad and brother years before and were still there, but almost buried from the windblown sand. As we went in the back door, it was like stepping back in time. The kitchen, with its white cotton curtains and wood cabinets still looked the same and was in surprisingly good shape. The counters were butcher block. My mother had those put in one year to replace the original laminate. The hardwood floors were worn from years of sandy feet, but they were clean. The management company knew we were coming, so they had cleaned everything. It was livable on the inside, just dated. My mother had worked hard to furnish each room with things that were special to our family: a shell, or a picture, or some treasure found on the beach. All of those treasures were there just as she left them, like a museum. I never expected it to be so hard. It was like she had simply stepped into the other room. Dad had not spoken. He was only walking from room to room, looking at things, touching each trinket. I came up beside him and asked if he remembered where mom had gotten the old iron mermaid that was on the shelf.

"No, I don't think I was with her when she bought that," he said. The truth was, he probably didn't know where she got anything in the entire house. He never went with her shopping. She would spend hours scouring small shops and antique stores for items that stood out to her and struck her fancy. Her taste was eclectic and she was very good at bringing various items into a room and making it seem like they went together. That's probably were I got my love for decorating and fixing up things that others would have considered trash. I think the entire house had refinished furniture or something she had painted.

I walked through the living room and out the door onto the porch and there it was...my place, the place I loved to spend every minute. I would read on that old swing until the sun went down and I couldn't see the words anymore. I ate my meals there and spent hours just sitting, daydreaming and listening to the ocean. Even if it rained, I could be found on that porch. I could smell the salt air and feel the wind blowing my hair. As a teenager, I hated that wind. I would fix my hair for a date and five minutes later it would be blown all over. But in that moment, it was wonderful. The water was blue and sparkled like diamonds forming a perfectly straight line against the white sand on one side and against the blue sky on the other. How could it not have changed over all those years and how was my love for it stronger than I had ever felt before. I couldn't wait to get out there.

"SAMMY, Sammy come here!" Dad yelled from inside. His voice interrupted me and I turned to see what he needed. My visit to the water would have to wait.

Dad was standing in the bathroom looking at the ceiling, or at the large hole in the ceiling. It looked like there had been a small water leak that had turned into a bigger problem. He blew out his breath in discouragement. Seeing the house made Dad look more tired than he did before we left home.

"Come on dad, let's find some supper and we can work on this later. We will take care of all these little issues, I promise." I loved my dad so much and we had gotten closer in the past year. I hated to see him sad or disappointed. We unpacked and decided to find an early supper before the sun went down.

The air was chilly, but still held that familiar feel of years past. It wasn't late, but being December, the day had already started to come to a close. The small town looked so empty compared to those busy summer memories in my head, but it looked nice all decorated for Christmas. Of course it wasn't decorated like most towns were for Christmas. Every decoration had a beach theme to it, but it was cute. We never visited in the winter, so this was so different.

"Dad! Look it's the ice cream shop! It's still here!"

There on the corner was the same little ice cream shop that we rode those bikes to as kids and teenagers. With its brightly colored walls and large polka dots, and now it had Christmas lights added to the colors. It looked like they had added coffee to their menu too. There were small tables outside to sit at and now the area had bistro lights strung across it for the evening customers.

"Well would you look at that", Dad said, pointing to the sign, "they have jumped on the specialty coffee wagon like everyone in the big city!"

"Yea, it looks like they have, but that's not a bad thing" I smiled back. I loved a good cup of coffee and besides bicycles and ice cream cones were not really a part of my life anymore. We went on down the street toward the hardware store and dad decided we should go in and get a few things before deciding on dinner. As we opened the door, a familiar face met us.

"Oh my goodness, it can't be! John Alexander, is that you or are these old eyes playing tricks on me?" said the older gentleman behind the counter.

My dad's eyes lit up brighter than I had seen them in months. "Joe? Joe Rogers? It can't be! Have you not been washed away in that old sail boat by now?" my dad said.

Both the old men grabbed each other's hands and the shake turned into a hug. My dad loved that hardware store. He probably should have been a handy man instead of an accountant. On vacation, when he was there with us, he spent a lot of his time fixing up the beach house and doing odd jobs on my mother's never ending "honey do" list. He and the owner became best buddies. I watched as they acted like two teenage boys, picking up right where they left off. The store owner's wife had also passed a few years ago, but two of his kids lived close by. Dad told him about the ceiling and that we would need some help with it. He said he knew a dependable guy and would send him by in the morning to take a look at it. We bought some light bulbs and headed out to find dinner. Joe recommended the little restaurant two doors down.

To be such a small town, they really went all out for Christmas. Christmas for us had become pretty small since mom had passed, so I had forgotten how pretty all the lights and trees were. It seemed like all the stores had that fake snow in the windows. Even though there were surf boards and sea shells on every corner, they all had Christmas lights and candy canes hanging on them. What could be nicer than the beach mixed with Christmas? I had forgotten how much I missed both. Mom made Christmas so special. She would fuss over every detail. Decorations, food, gifts, and cookies, oh the cookies! We had to decorate them every year. They didn't always look great, but she made it a point to keep our family together. Somehow when we lost her, we lost that too. Maybe we should make cookies again! *I hear you mom*, I thought, as I glanced upward. Maybe, as usual, she still knew just what we needed.

I thought the restaurant was surprisingly crowded for a winter evening and it smelled heavenly. The waitress motioned for us to take a booth near the door. My dad never meets a stranger so he had to tell her that we were here for Christmas and that the "whole" family was coming! She acted like we were her only customers and talked to my dad like an old friend. She told us to be sure and bring the kids to the Pier City Christmas Carnival a few days before Christmas. Dad had meatloaf and mashed potatoes that he swore was almost as good as moms. I had baked chicken and a salad.

It was dark by the time we got back to the beach house and the wind from the ocean was blowing strong when we got out of the car. I could see the waves with the reflection of the moon. We went in and turned the heat up, but decided against building a fire until we got the fireplace checked. Dad settled into one of the old chairs that he always loved and was soon sound asleep. It had been a long trip and a long day. I was tired too, but I just had to get a closer look.

I wondered back onto the screen porch and could see the white crests of the waves stirred up by the wind. It was cold, so I threw on my coat and hat and headed down the path toward the beach. It wasn't far down that familiar little trail until I was standing in the wide open. As my eyes adjusted, I could see for what seemed like miles in every direction. I had forgotten how vast and beautiful it was. It's impossible to see that far in a city. The wind was roaring and the waves were crashing onto the sand. They weren't huge waves, but big enough for me to hear them from a distance. So strange how it was all consuming. How small it made me feel, yet somehow complete. I could have stood there for hours. There must have been a million stars. You never see stars like that where I live with all the city lights! After a while, I realized how cold it was, so I turned to head back inside. Hopefully the sun would warm things up and I could go for a long walk tomorrow. I decided to just let dad rest in that chair and covered him up with a blanket. There was a little mermaid on my bedside table that my mother had bought years before. She always told me that the mermaid would help me dream about my happiest days! I fell asleep thinking of her. The bright sun startled me out of a dream..that mermaid was a big disappointment. I was dreaming about Kyle Martin and a fun sunny day on the beach. Where in the world had that come from? I sat up, opened the bedside drawer and tossed the mermaid into it. *Sorry Mom, no mermaid dreams for this girl!* He was the last thing I wanted to be dreaming about.

CHAPTER 7

Making sure we had coffee was great idea because I needed a cup first thing. I decided I should make a list for the handy man guy of the things that needed to be done before everyone arrived. The ceiling had to be fixed for sure and the screens on the porch. The fireplace needed to be checked, but most everything else was just general clean up and landscaping, unless he saw something wrong. Did handy men do landscaping or did I need a landscape man too? None of these decisions are required for condo life. Anyway, I would make the list and he could tell me what he could and would do. I also needed help with a Christmas tree at some point, if I was going to keep my promise to Mac and his girls and to my dad.

I poured my second cup of coffee and found Dad on the porch on Mom's swing.

"She sure did love this old thing", he said.

"Yes, she did," I agreed. "I think she even slept there a few times."

My dad had this huge swing built for my mom to hang on the porch. It was as big as a small bed. It was her spot to relax, but we all got to hang out there. There were fans on the porch when it was hot and blankets on the swing when it was cold. It seemed like we ended up there every morning for coffee and every evening to watch the sun go down. Life was slower here, and I liked it that way.

"You know, I can almost feel her here," Dad said, "like she's just in that kitchen making breakfast or down there on the beach taking a walk."

"Yea, me too, Dad. It's nice. I haven't felt this way in a long, long time. I really love this old place."

"You always loved the beach as much as your mother did. I think you would have lived here if we would have let you. Especially when you met that boy. What was his name? Kyle Something?" Dad said with a smirk.

I laughed, "That was a long time ago, a lifetime ago. We were kids. What was I supposed to do just quit school and let your business go to some stranger?"

"Sammy, you need your own dreams. Now go take that walk!"

"Ok, I will be back before the guy comes. I won't be long."

The sun was up and warm on my face, but the morning wind still felt cool. The sand was just like I remembered, soft and white like powder. It was breathtaking! Seagulls swooped down to see if I had brought breakfast with me, but there was hardly anyone on the beach except a few people walking their dogs.

I love dogs, but I hadn't had my own dog since we were kids. About the closest I came was the summer here at the beach with Kyle. We had the bright idea to adopt a puppy. Her big brown sad eyes won me over first thing and I convinced him that we should take her. We named her Sally and called her Sal. She was a golden retriever, loved the beach and the water and chewed up everything. When I left that summer, he promised to take good care of her, but I never saw her again. I missed her horribly, but I had to go. I had those responsibilities hanging on my shoulders.

Reluctantly, I turned to walk back toward the house, wishing I could spend the day there, but I didn't want to miss the handy man or leave him to meet with just my dad. Lord knows what he would have him doing. I got almost to my path and noticed someone's dog had gotten lose and was bounding straight for me! And was not slowing down! Their owner was chasing behind yelling for them to STOP, SIT, STAY! But the dog didn't stop, sit or stay. It came straight at me and jumped right into my chest, knocking me over in the sand. It didn't hurt, but I was caught off guard. I let out a scream but she continued to stand over me licking my face like I was her long lost friend. The owner came running up.

"Sal, what on earth are you doing? NO! You know better! Get off of her!"

But she didn't get off of me, she just kept licking my face and barking at him.

"Sal?" I opened my eyes. It couldn't be. The sun was in my face but the owner had gotten his dog off me and was trying to help me up.

"Sammy? Is that you?" the guy said.

I looked up and shaded my eyes to see. "Kyle? Kyle Martin?

I couldn't believe my eyes. He was standing right in front of me after 7 years. I was shocked and covered in sand from the dog pouncing. I didn't know what to say or where to begin. He looked just as handsome as he ever did, but I looked like I had just rolled out of bed. I had expected to see a handy man, not the guy I was supposed to marry, and if I did see him, it was not supposed to be like this.

"How are you?" I managed to stammer out, "is this Sal?" She was still licking and panting and running around me. He said he was fine and that was indeed Sal, Sally, that little puppy from many summers ago. He swore somehow she seemed to remember me. I doubted that, but it did warm my heart to think she might. I reached down to pet her head and she licked me again.

"So what are you doing back here after so long? I don't think you've been back one time since ....." his voice trailed off.

"Oh.. umm, my dad hasn't been feeling well and he insisted that the family spend Christmas here at the old house.

Who knows, probably our last time to visit here. I think we will probably put it up for sale after the holidays since we never come back anymore. I came early to get things in order before Lizzy and Mac get here. I was just coming to meet a handy man that's supposed to come by and help with a few projects." I was rambling.

"Well, that would be me", he laughed, "I'm your guy...well not *your guy,* I'm the handyman and it would be a shame to sell this great house so close to the water. I have actually worked on the outside of this house several times over the past couple of years patching up things here and there, putting on shutters for storms, and stuff like that."

"Oh, you're the guy, then? You do handyman work? Ok, well, I guess I can show you a couple of things."

We made awkward small talk as he looked at the house issues. I was surprised that he did this for a living. He had great plans to be a successful architect. He wanted to remodel old buildings and maybe design some of his own. I guess I wasn't the only one whose plans had done a 360. My dad was so happy to see him and winked at me like I was still in high school and had just brought by first boyfriend home to meet him. Sal, well, she quickly became my dad's new best pal. Kyle walked through and looked in each room to see what needed to be done.

"Man, it's been a long time since I was in here, but honestly it looks almost the same," he commented.

He agreed that the house needed a good bit of work, and he wouldn't be able to finish it all before Christmas, but it was still a great house. Because it was off season, he would be able to get to it pretty fast and he could actually start later that afternoon.

"Wow, that's soon, are you sure you aren't too busy? I mean it can wait until tomorrow."

So he was a handyman and not a very busy one, which would be normal in this small town. I just thought he would do more with his life.

"No, I'm good. There's quite a bit to be done before your family arrives. I should get on it pretty fast. I will see you after lunch, Sammy", he winked.

I smiled and agreed and felt a weird flip in my stomach. Probably because I hadn't been winked in seven years. That boy and those blue eyes and that wink always got to me, but I wasn't twenty years old now. I was a grown woman with a career and a life, well sort of a life, but I wasn't a silly girl falling for a wink! What had I gotten myself into? I would have never in a million years expected to see Kyle Martin at my house again. I would never thought he would even speak if he ever saw me in public again, but he did.

It seems as though, parts of our past, some good and some bad, just stand, face pressed against the glass waiting for that single moment to rush back into our lives. They are forever reminding us of the things we put behind us so long ago. Full circle, my mom used to say.

CHAPTER 8

It was a warm sunny afternoon, so dad and I fixed lunch and ate on the porch. Even with the broken screens, it was wonderful. The afternoon breeze blowing and the view of the water was so calming to me. I loved this porch and the peace it brought to me and it was going to be my first project. We were still eating when Kyle drove up in his truck, Sal bounding from the back. She was determined to win me over again. It was like she didn't even care that I left. She was just happy that I was in her life again. This time she sat politely beside my chair wiggling all over until I conceded and began to pet her. After a couple of big slurps up my face with her tongue, she was content to see if dad had any snacks left over from lunch. I asked Kyle if he could please fix the screens on the porch first, as he was pulling screen material from his truck.

"Great minds," he laughed.

"I'm going to start with this porch and get it fixed up. It's my favorite spot of the house," I said.

"Always was," he agreed, "and your Mom's too if I remember correctly. I sure was sorry to hear about her passing Sammy. She was a great woman and she sure loved this town and this house."

"Thanks, yea she did. I think she passed that on to me. I forgot how great it is here." He smiled and kept unloading his truck. I wondered what he thought about seeing me again. I wondered if he had missed me when I left.

"Ok, I'm going to town to see if I can find a cover for this old swing. Dad will be here if you need anything."

I decided to walk the short walk to town because it was so beautiful out. I needed a jacket, but the sun was warming me up as long as I stayed out of the shade.

I stopped for a coffee at the ice cream shop, found a coverlet and a couple of pillows at one of the antique stores and stopped back by the hardware store for some spray paint to freshen up the chairs. I was once again greeted by my dad's old friend. He loved to talk and told me how my parents had always planned to move there someday, but dad just kept getting busier and busier and we grew up and got our own lives and that they eventually stopped coming all together. He had thought they would retire there.

I thanked him as I left, but I thought about what he said on my way back. It made me sad to think about how life had gotten in the way of my parent's dreams. How my dad had worked so hard to take care of us and be there for us, then when it was their turn, it was too late. I was glad that I brought him here. I was glad that we were having Christmas at the beach house, and I was sure my mom was smiling on me, or maybe laughing at the sight of my face when Kyle showed up.

The warm sun had started slipping away as I got closer to home and the evening breeze picked up. It was pretty cool walking back, but the sound of the crashing waves made it worth being cold. I hated to even think about work while I was here. No reason to think about accounting, I had work to do on the house and I loved every minute of it. I came through the front door to see Kyle on a ladder, my dad in his chair and Sal stretched out in front of the fireplace with a warm fire burning.

"Kyle! The fireplace! It may not be safe!"

"Sammy, do you think I would build a fire in a fireplace that I didn't check first?" he asked.

"I don't know" I said, "I would hope not."

"Well, you're right, you don't know, but I wouldn't. Your dad was chilly, so I went ahead and checked out the fireplace and built him a little fire. He fell fast asleep, but I'm making enough noise to wake the dead." he laughed.

"Don't worry, you won't wake him. And the fire feels great!" Sal nuzzled her nose into my hand for a quick hello and curled back up at dad's feet to finish her nap.

I took my stuff straight through the house and onto the porch. The screens were fixed and looked great. I swept and mopped the floor, changed the cover on the swing, knocked down the cobwebs and wiped down the furniture. Painting would have to wait until morning, but it already looked better. I was pleased with it and Mom would have been too. The sun was setting as I went back inside and Kyle was picking up the mess from the leaky ceiling. He didn't notice me watching him. It was odd to see him fast forwarded so many years into the future, the same but different. At one point, we knew each other's thoughts and now I knew literally nothing about him. He wasn't wearing a wedding ring. Was he divorced, widowed, still single like me? He was tan even in the middle of winter. Perks of living at the beach year round I suppose. Still blond haired and blue eyed and still handsome. I broke his heart when I left and one thing I did know about him, he was not one to open up and take chances with people again. Sal caught me watching and jumped up to greet me. "Hey girl, did you have a good nap? It's time for some dinner!"

"She would sleep all day if she could get away with it. She's getting' older, not that little puppy anymore." He said, reminding me.

"Well, we're all a little older now aren't we Sal? Hey Dad, you ready for dinner?" I changed the subject.

Dad was starving and so was I and it was getting late.

"Hey, you guys want to try a new restaurant over on the bay? My treat!" Kyle asked.

"Umm, it's kind of late and I don't know ..." I was squirming for an answer, but Dad interrupted,

"Sure! Sounds fantastic, doesn't it Sammy?"

"Sure Dad, fantastic." Could my day get any more awkward?

We left Sal at the house and headed toward the bay with Kyle driving us like a tour guide pointing out all the new places and changes in the town. Dad could have listened to him for hours, but I just sat in the back seat trying to figure out what time warp I had stepped in to. I hardly heard a word he said. He just kept glancing in the review mirror to see if I was listening. I wasn't, but I smiled back politely. I wasn't being rude, it was nice to see him, I just never expected to it at all. Then he shows up at my house working with the dog we shared. Now he is driving me around town chatting with my dad, like no time has passed at all. It was just weird, oddly, nicely weird.

The Fish Fin was a hole in the wall restaurant with a gorgeous view of the pink bay sky and oddly enough it was pretty crowded. It was decorated with a nice beach theme mixed with a little bit of Christmas. We only waited a few minutes to be seated at a table by the window. Kyle pulled out my chair, then sat beside me and Dad sat across from us.

"Man oh man, look at that sunset over the water, Sammy! Isn't it great?"

"Yea, it's really nice Dad, so pretty!" I managed to say.

But I could only think about the fact that he was sitting three inches from me. I was over reacting. This was silly. We were grown adults having dinner, nothing else, old friends, acquaintances. Except that we were almost engaged and I changed the entire plan with the drop of a hat and left him high and dry and never looked back. Now I'm making small talk over crab claws! Ok, pull it together Sammy, before he thinks you're crazy.

"So Kyle, did you ever get married?" I heard my dad ask. Surely I heard wrong! I glared at him across the table.

"No, I didn't ever marry. Just me and Sal working on houses. I went on to college and got a degree in architecture, but no, never married."

Dad loved that, "Really? Sammy has never married either!"

"Architecture? Really, that's so interesting", I interrupted, "so why do you just do handyman work? I mean, I guess that sounded rude. Sorry."

"No", he smiled, "it wasn't rude at all. I graduated and moved inland and worked for a big company. I lived in the city and made good money. It was a dream job, I guess, but not my dream job."

"Seems like a great job to me," I said.

He paused and looked me right in the eye,

"I wanted to be here, to live here every day. I missed the water and the smell of the salt air. Some things you just can't buy no matter how good the job is, Sammy."

"So what's for dinner tonight?" the waitress had saved me.

We ate as we watched the last bit of sun slide into the ocean. There are no sunsets like that in the city where I live. If there are, they must be hidden behind trees or buildings. I remembered that it was my favorite time of the day. No picture or painting can actually capture the beauty of it.

Dinner was wonderful and we chatted about my mom and brother and sister and their families. Kyle's parents were still alive and still lived in this same town, but he had bought a house on the beach out of town away from the tourists where the locals go. A "fixer upper", he called it. I was curious to see it, but I would never ask. I would be leaving right after Christmas. No time to get involved and I would never take the chance of hurting him again. But we had always talked about buying an old cottage and working our charm on it.

We arrived back at the beach to be greeted by sleeping Sal. We thanked Kyle for dinner and he said he would see us in the morning to continue working on the ceiling. I followed him to the door to lock it behind him and Sal. He paused for a moment, "it's really great to see you again Sammy", he said with a wink.

"You too," I looked away, almost blushing, "see you tomorrow." He turned and left and I locked the door. That wink! He really needed to stop that.

CHAPTER 9

I'm up with the sun at the shore, always have been. At home, I hit the snooze button five times and still drag myself out of bed to the shower, but when I'm at the beach, the sun wakes me up. I feel rested and ready to go. Mom and I would always get up before everyone else, make our coffee and head to the beach for a long walk before it was invaded by swimmers and sunbathers. Sometimes we even beat the sunrise, and got to watch it come up over the water. Somehow, it was the loudest quiet place on earth. The crashing waves sometimes so loud, yet I could close my eyes and hear the quietness of my thoughts better than I could anywhere else. The vastness of the ocean seemed to put life into perspective for me.

Dad was up and already had coffee brewing when I made it to the kitchen. I saw him sitting outside with a blanket on Mom's swing. He missed her, but was doing okay. His face lit up when I opened the creaky screen door.

"Sammy, the porch looks like a new place! I know your mom is smiling in heaven today! What's today's project?" he asked.

"Well, I'm taking a walk on the beach first, then I'm going to give these old chairs a coat of paint. Then, I'm going to spruce up the living room and kitchen I think."

"I think I need a nap already," he laughed. "I think you could make this place your home, Sammy. Your mother always wanted that. The whole family liked it, but you two, loved it. She would work on this beach house all summer and dreamed of living here. I really hate to think about getting rid of the old place."

"Let's don't think about it Dad, let's enjoy it and celebrate Christmas!" I smiled, but it broke my heart to think about selling this house.

It was filling up a piece of my heart that I didn't even know I was missing. I had put it out of my mind for so long and tried to move forward with my life that I thought it had all gone away, but being here again brought it all back. All the love that I had for this place was right back in my heart and I couldn't bear to think about losing it again. I gave him a quick kiss on the cheek and headed for the beach. He touched his face and I realized I probably hadn't kissed his cheek like that in years. Oh well, it was a beautiful day at the shore and that made me extra happy.

My walk was full of treasures. That's what Mom called them. Pieces of drift wood, odd shells, sea glass or anything she thought she might be able to use to craft something else out of. I found a great piece of driftwood and a shell that was perfect, not broken at all. Of course the house did not need another piece of drift wood or one more shell, but I couldn't just leave these perfect treasures on the beach. I talked to a couple of friendly dogs out for their morning strolls and I took a moment to notice how many new homes there were along the shore that weren't there before. My coffee cup was empty, so I headed back to the house looking down at the sand for more treasures. I heard a dog bark and looked up to see Sal bounding toward me again, but this time I was able to brace myself for her love leap. She licked my face and ran in circles around my legs.

"Good morning!" Kyle flashed a smile, "I brought donuts!"

"You did? I love donuts!" I reached for the box. I let my guard down for a second, but in all fairness, I had not had breakfast.

"Yea, I remember," he said, holding it out of my reach, "these are for your dad!"

"What? Give me those! I will share with him."

"Doubtful," he teased, as he brought the box within reach. I grabbed the box and ran toward the porch. "Dad, Kyle brought donuts!"

I fixed a second cup of coffee and we had donuts on the porch. It was cold out, but we didn't care because the view was so great. Dad went inside after a few minutes and left Kyle and I alone.

"Well, I better get started on my chairs," I said, trying to find a reason to leave.

"Wait, Sammy, can we talk for a minute?" he asked, "you owe me that much."

"Ok, yea sure." I said, not knowing how this might go.

"I just need to know, why did you do it? Why did you leave like you did?" he looked my straight in the eye. I wanted to look away, but I tried not to.

"We made plans together, we were on the same page I thought, and then you just left. No warning, no conversation, no explanation, just like what we had didn't mean anything at all."

He was right, I did leave the wrong way and he did deserve an answer, but I couldn't give him one because I didn't know myself.

He waited and I said nothing.

"Well, you're not even going to answer?" he asked.

Before I could come up with the words, he stood up and turned to walk off.

"Kyle, wait!" He stopped with his back to me. "I don't know why", I said.

"Really, this much time has passed and you haven't even thought about it enough to know why you did it?" He walked into the house and let the screen slam.

I knew why, but I didn't. I had reasons, but when I said them out loud or wrote them down like I had done so many times in letters to send to him, they just sounded foolish. They seemed like important reasons until I heard them with my own ears, then they seemed like the easy way out for a girl that didn't want to rock the boat. A girl that didn't want to tell her parents that her dreams and theirs didn't match. A girl that felt like she had to be the one to take care of her parents or no one else would. Maybe a girl just too afraid to do her own thing. I didn't know how to tell him all those things. How could I tell him that all of that was more important than him, or convince him that I was too dumb and young to realize how important he was.

The ringing phone disrupted my spinning thoughts. It was Lizzy on the other end.

"Hey Sis, how's it going? Lizzy asked, "You getting anything done. Is the house in shambles?"

"Hey!" I tried to sound happy, "everything is okay here. The house is pretty good. There are a few things that need some work. The weather is nice and the beach is as beautiful as ever! I can't wait for you to see it!"

"Yea, and all that sand getting everywhere too, I can't wait for that either", Lizzy said, sarcastically. "What do you mean the house needs work, what's wrong with the house?"

"Oh, just a few repairs, nothing major, and maybe some sprucing up!" I lied, sort of.

"Sammy, please tell me you and dad are not trying to do all this stuff by yourselves. He is supposed to be resting and you have to run the business even if you are out of town."

"No, Lizzy, we hired someone to do the work." I stepped outside so Kyle couldn't hear me. "He is here now working on a small leak in the roof.

"Ooh, is he single? Oh is he old?" Lizzy asked, always hoping to fix me up with someone.

"Uh...No, he isn't old and yes, I believe he is single, but I'm not looking for anything to happen with anyone here, Lizzy," I said flatly.

"Come on Sammy, give the guy a chance! Is he ugly?" she pried.

"Well, no, I can't say that he is ugly either." I answered.

"Saaammmy! Have you not even asked the guy his name?"

"Oh my gosh, Lizzy, yes I know his name. His name is Kyle Martin! There, are you happy? I know his name, and pretty much anything else you would want to know about him!"

Silence.

"Oh no, Sammy! Not *THE Kyle Martin*?"

"Yep, that's the one. Oh, and he has Sal with him every single day. Last night, dad accepted a dinner invite for both of us to go out to eat with him and this morning, he brought donuts, confronted me about why I left, and I just stood there staring at him. Needless to say, he stormed off mad. So yea, what else would you like to know about the repair man?"

She could hear my voice quiver.

"Sammy are you ok? I'm so sorry, that must be horrible. Who would ever have thought that he would still be there?"

I composed myself and said, "Well, I have to admit, I did wonder if he was still living close by, but I definitely didn't expect him to show up on the porch with our dog and a tool box. It's a lot and I feel like I'm in a time warp or something. When are you coming?"

"Christmas is on a Friday, so I'm going to try to get there sometime earlier in the week. Will you be okay?"

"Yes, I'm going to work on the house and I have to be in touch with the office tomorrow, so I have plenty to keep my busy. Besides, you know I always loved it here. I didn't realize how much I missed this being in my life. I will figure out the rest somehow."

"Okay, Sammy, I will see you as soon as I can" she promised. "And Sammy?"

"Yea?"

"Maybe you should just talk to him, maybe you should just lay it all out there and look at it even if it hurts. Maybe it's been long enough."

"Yea, maybe." I said quietly, "I love you, see you in a couple of weeks."

Talk to him? Long enough? Where would I even begin? We weren't kids anymore and it wasn't like I was trying to fix a break up or anything. I just needed to give him the explanation he wanted and needed and that would be that. Now if I could just come up with that explanation, we could just move on. The problem was that all of the reasons that seemed so important at the time, just seemed like lame excuses now. Is that why he had never married? Did it break his heart that bad? Did he wait for me? That's silly, right? Wait, is that why I never married? My heart was so sad when I left. I would never have let myself care like that again.

CHAPTER 10

Kyle and Dad were talking about the roof when I went back into the kitchen. He ignored me walking by and kept talking. Dad looked at us both, but said nothing which was a miracle.

I had decided that the living room would be my project that day, but it would probably take a couple of days to be honest. The shelves had old books and magazines that needed to be cleaned off. There was a wooden chest full of junk to be cleaned out and the entire room needed a good cleaning. The furniture wasn't new but we had replaced it a few years ago when the rental company had said the other stuff was just getting too worn out. My parents bought a new sofa and love seat, but dad's old chair stayed there and an old wooden mission chair that my mom loved, but it needed some cushion help.

Kyle told my dad that the roof would need a patch on the outside, some work in the attic, and then the ceiling would need to be patched and fixed inside. It would take a few days. Meanwhile, Dad had found several more jobs for him to be working on. The kitchen sink was leaking and so was one of the toilets. A few of the storm shutters were broken and needed to be replaced. The bushes needed to be cut back and trimmed around the house and the linoleum was coming loose in the kitchen. What in the world? Was he just trying to think of ways to keep him coming back? I was going through old books and Kyle was working in the kitchen. You could have heard a pin drop when my dad came in from the yard.

"Hey Kyle, anywhere around here have a nice Christmas tree and some decorations?" he asked.

Kyle glanced at me, "Well, there's a lot downtown that sells trees. I'm sure they have some nice ones."

"Yea, what about decorations?" Dad pressed, "Where can we get those? The grand kids are coming and we need a tree, a big pretty one with lots of lights."

"Dad?" I laughed "what on earth has gotten into you? You haven't put up a tree in years!"

Kyle smiled back.

"I know, I know!" Dad said, "But it just feels right this year. It feels like that's what we should be doing, you know, for the kids."

"Now where is this place, Kyle? Can you take us in your truck?"

"Dad, I'm sure Kyle has better things to do than drive us all over town looking for Christmas trees. We can handle it on our own." I was trying to help the awkwardness, but Dad nor Kyle were helping.

"What are you going to do, tie it to the top of your little car?" Kyle quipped.

"Well, I could. Maybe." I really had no idea if that was possible or not.

"Nonsense," Dad joined in, "Kyle can run us over, can't you, son?"

"I guess I can," he said, looking at me like there was no way out.

I was sure he didn't want to be stuck with us anymore than I wanted to go Christmas tree shopping with him, but Dad had made up his mind. At least Sal was happy to get to tag along this time.

It was only about three weeks until Christmas, but there was still a pretty good selection of trees on the lot. The sun was setting and it was cold. Strange it being cold at the beach, but I was freezing. Kyle walked up and threw his jacket around me. I only had on a light jacket and he could see that I was freezing.

"Oh, I'm good, you don't have to do that."

"Just stop, Sammy! You're freezing and it's just a jacket," he said quietly.

Kyle was a nice guy. He was always very thoughtful and always made sure I was taken care of. He was a gentleman for sure. I guess that had not changed. His jacket was warm and smelled really nice too. I remembered his father being really nice to his mother. I guess he passed that down to Kyle.

"How about this one, Sammy?" Dad yelled. He was holding a nine foot tree that would take up half the living room of the beach house.

"Dad, isn't that a little too big for the living room?" I laughed and elbowed Kyle to make him look.

"Whoa, that's a big one," Kyle yelled, "Maybe Sammy could tie that on her car!"

I hit him, "You hush! My car is great!"

He busted out laughing, "Yeah maybe so, but not for hauling trees! Yea, that looks liked a great tree, but I think you may have to move the furniture out of the living room to set it up in there."

He had not laughed since I had been here, not a real laugh. That laugh would make me smile on my worst of days. His laugh made me laugh, every time. He caught himself and remembered that he was still upset with me.

"Better help your Dad find a tree that will fit inside the house." He said and walked off.

I had to figure out what to say and how to say it, in a way that wouldn't be hurtful all over again. The hard part was trying to figure out myself why I even did it in the first place. Seeing him again was beginning to make all those good reasons seem more ridiculous.

Somehow he talked my Dad into a five foot tree and some lights and we were finally back inside the warm truck. I realized on the way back, that we didn't have any decorations, so we stopped at a small store in town and got a few boxes of Christmas balls and a tree stand. I picked out a few special decorations that I thought the girls might like to put on the tree too.

Kyle unloaded the tree for us and he and Dad put it in the stand while I threw together some spaghetti for dinner.

"Want to stay for some spaghetti?" I asked. "You're welcome to stay. There's plenty." I felt bad for hurting his feelings and didn't want him to leave like that.

"No, I think I will head on home," he said. I knew he still had his guard up and with good reason.

"Oh no you don't! You're not leaving me here with him and those boxes of lights." I said, nodding my head toward my dad, who had already managed to pull the lights out of the boxes and tangle them.

He smiled, "How did he already do that?"

"I don't know, but it will take me till midnight to put those things on the tree with him. Let's eat first, then put them on. Then you can leave, I promise."

"Hey Dad, let's eat, then we will put the lights on the tree, okay?"

"Oh alright, the way they cram these things in the boxes, I think they must be in a mess before you even buy them."

"Well, Sammy can put them on for you," Kyle said, sarcastically.

We sat at the table and ate my best spaghetti, bread and salad and Kyle built a fire in the fireplace. It was so warm and cozy, Sal found her favorite spot on the rug and fell asleep. Under Dad's supervision, we were able to get all the lights on the tree without killing him or each other.

While we were hanging the balls on the tree, Dad disappeared into the bedroom. In a few minutes he returned with a box that had a lid on it that was taped shut. He brought it from home, but I never asked what was in it. He sat down and looked at me, and pulled the tape off the box. It was full of ornaments.

Our old Christmas ornaments that mom had saved over the years. The ones that were special to her, that she would hang on the tree every year. They had not been unpacked since the Christmas before she passed. Every year, she would give us a new ornament of something that she thought we would like. Some of the ornaments had been given to us when we moved out and had our own Christmas trees, but some were still in that box.

"Dad? It's Mom's ornaments." I looked at Kyle. "We haven't used these since she passed away.

"It's time to use them again, Sammy. Your mom would want them to be here. She would want us to enjoy them here." He had tears in his eyes.

"Dad, she would love that. I'm so glad you brought them."

"Maybe I should go and leave you two alone." Kyle said from across the room.

"No, you don't have to go," I said.

"Absolutely not," Dad agreed. "She would be quite happy that you were here taking care of her house. Now let's get these on the tree."

We placed each ornament carefully on the tree and I shared with Kyle the story behind each one. Most of them were funny stories of me and Mac and Lizzy.

Soon Dad was fast asleep in his chair and the decorations were left to Kyle and me. It was quiet, but not awkward, more like a comfortable. It shouldn't have felt that way at all, but it did.

"Got to admit this is pretty weird," he broke the silence.

"What's that?" I asked, but I knew.

"I just never thought in a million years we would be here decorating a Christmas tree this many years later...never would have thought it."

"Kyle," I said quietly, "you deserve an answer."

He interrupted, "Sammy, just don't worry about it. All that was a long time ago and it's over now. You don't owe me anything."

"Yes, I do. It was forever ago it seems like, but you still deserve an answer to your question otherwise it feels like it all didn't mean anything and it did mean something." He didn't speak. He just stared at me, waiting.

"That summer meant everything to me. You meant everything to me, but the pressure to go back home and finish school so I could run my father's business was so big, so heavy. My brother had already hurt Dad so deeply by deciding to start his own business and Lizzy was always going to do what Lizzy wanted. I felt like my parents future depended on my decision. There was no room for what I wanted. I didn't even know how to consider myself because I only knew how to think about what would work for everyone else. Then there was you, wanting me to stay here and live a dream that I wasn't even sure could work. I knew I could never see you and be able to leave, so I just left. I knew you would move on and build a life and so would I. I'm so sorry I did it that way, I just didn't know what to do."

He just stood there looking at me, not saying a word.

"I know it sounds dumb and lame," I started again, "I knew it would. I said it out loud a million times over all these years trying to make it sound like I did the right thing and it always sounds the same."

"Shhh...stop talking," he whispered, stepping closer. "It doesn't sound dumb or lame. It sounds like a young girl feeling pressure from every side including from the guy that was supposed to love her. You should have been able to tell me anything, not have to carry all that on your shoulders alone. You left me and Sal and went home, finished school and started a career that you didn't want to make sure your parents were okay. Yea, I wish you could have talked to me, but I guess I can see why you couldn't. I wish you would have given me the chance to be there to help you."

"I know, so do I." I said. "Looking back, I would have done it all differently. Somehow, I would have found a different way."

"I should probably go. It's getting late." He said quietly.

"Oh, ok, yea, that's fine." I was surprised.

"Hey, can I show you something tomorrow? Maybe in the morning?" he asked.

"Um, yea, I guess so. What is it?"

"You'll see!" he smiled, as he headed out the door. "I'll pick you up at nine."

I knew from his smile that he wasn't upset with me anymore. Maybe he understood, and maybe I understood finally too. I wondered if we could move forward as friends. I wondered what the future might hold for us.

Mom always told me that some things take minutes to work out and some things take years, but if we trust and pray, they will always find a way to work out. Tonight I knew just what she meant.

CHAPTER 11

I woke up early, jumped out of bed and looked for something to wear, in my limited supply of clothes. I didn't have anything that looked great. I didn't expect to need anything that looked good for going out. Why was I worried anyway? It wasn't a big event or a date… *A DATE*? No, definitely not a date. I threw on some sweats and running shoes and headed for the kitchen for coffee. I wanted to get my walk on the beach in before Kyle got there to pick me up. I had no idea what he wanted to show me, but I figured I owed him that much and besides I was curious at this point.

I put a lid on my coffee and started down the path toward the beach, when I saw my dad already down by the ocean. How did he get up and out of the house without me hearing him? I had never even seen him take walks on the beach. My mom did every day, but dad was always too busy. Too rushed to enjoy it the way she did.

"Dad! What are you doing out so early this morning?" I yelled above the waves.

"Just decided to go for a little walk myself this morning. What are you doing? Thought Kyle was picking you up."

"He is, at nine. I just wanted to come down here with my coffee for a little bit. Do you have any idea what he wants to show me?"

"Me? No, no idea at all." He smiled. Pretty sure he was lying, but I left it alone.

"Well, I don't think I believe you, but okay."

"Hey Sammy, do you miss being here? Like really miss it, like your mother did when you all would come home after the summer? She would talk about it for weeks after that and count the days until she could come back. It seems like you have that same love for this place."

"I do love it Dad, probably almost as much as mom, but I have to remember that we have a life at home and I have a business to manage...that I need to call and check on today actually. This isn't my life here."

"Well, you seem more alive here than anywhere else, so maybe your life should be here. Maybe it's time for you to find another life. One that suits you better."

"We both know that's not possible, Dad. We will have Christmas, then go back to our normal life."

"Sammy, your life should not be 'our life'. Your life should be yours and maybe someone else's with you. Not mine and yours. Now I love you, and I appreciate you, but you can't keep living your life for me."

"Dad, where is all this coming from?" I was confused, and a little surprised. My dad's business had always come first. That's why I had left the beach to begin with. Now, all of the sudden, he talked like none of it mattered.

"I'm just saying, you should be able to live your life without worrying about me or a business that you have never even enjoyed! I know you only work there because you felt responsible for keeping it going, but I realized with your mother passing, life just isn't long enough to be living it for someone else's dream." When did my dad learn to see right through me? I didn't love my job or living the life I chose, but it was the only life I knew now, the only life I had.

I heard Kyle's truck horn and Sal barking and I knew this conversation would have to wait until later. I walked Dad back up to the house and left Sal to keep him company.

CHAPTER 12

The morning air was crisp and cool as Kyle turned and headed out of town.

"So where are we going? You can tell me now." I teased.

"Nope, just wait and see, nosey!" He knew I loved surprises, well he used to know. He used to know everything about me.

We rode out of town toward a small beach that only the locals know about. We went there in the summer when the beaches were packed with tourists. There were small houses that sat on one side of the road with big trees, but only the beach was on the other side of the tiny street. I used to dream of living there and fixing up one of those houses one day. They were old, but so charming.

"Man, it's changed a little out this way, but these old houses are still here."

"Yea, most of these are privately owned, so no rentals or tourists out this way. It has pretty much stayed the same over the years, except for owners remodeling and fixing up the original houses, and a couple of small restaurants. I have done quite a bit of work on this street." He said.

"Oh really?" I asked. "So a lot of people hire you for handy man work?"

"Yea, you could say that, I guess," he smiled.

"And, what does that mean?"

"I went to college and finished my degree in architecture and I used it for a while. Some people hire me for their remodels and expansion projects or even building from the ground up. I just don't do it for a big company anymore, I do it for my neighbors, I guess you could say. The handy man stuff is on the side, just to help people out and usually I have a couple of guys that do that for me, but they are busy right now with another house."

I wasn't surprised. He had always been a hard worker and always went the extra mile in everything he did. He was a perfectionist and loved working with his hands, or at least he did several years ago. He didn't seem to have changed too much. I used to know everything about him too.

The street was so pretty, just like I remembered it. The moss hung from the old trees and blew in the ocean breeze. The yards had pretty green grass, but twenty feet away was the beautiful white sand. The lucky owners could sit on the front porches and watch the sun rise over the ocean each morning on one side and watch it set on the other side, like a movie, and fall asleep to sound of the waves. The Christmas season had added decorations and lights to the street and most of the houses had trees decorated and wreaths on the doors. It brought back all the feelings of my love for that town, and some new feelings. I couldn't quite put my finger on it, but almost like being homesick.

We were almost at the end of the street when he slowed down and began to turn into one of the little driveways. The owner's had laid red brick pavers all the way to the garage and the grass grew down the center of the drive. The house had been updated but still had the original small beach bungalow style. They had added a garage and possibly a second story. The porch was something out of a magazine with bistro lights and a beautiful swing. The front door was solid wood with glass panes. It was so inviting, like being home.

"Wow, is this one of the houses you worked on? It's amazing. I have always loved this street and these old houses. A part of me wanted to decorate and design the interiors, you know, add art work and décor that makes them a home." I was amazed at the work he had done.

"I do remember you wanting to do that and I did do quite a bit of work on this house. Would you like to see the inside?" he asked.

"You still have a key? Yes, I would love to!" I said excitedly. "Is anyone home?"

"No, we can go inside, it's fine." He reached to open the door and I stepped in.

I stopped just inside the door to take it all in. The floors were original wide planks but had been refinished in a driftwood grey. The décor had some beach items but nothing tacky. There were paintings on the walls of blue waters and sailboats, a deep cotton covered sofa and oversized chair accented with turquoise. It was a dream. The kitchen had all the bells and whistles and had been completely remodeled.

"Does someone live here or is it a vacation rental?" I asked.

"Someone lives here. I'm actually still working on this house in my spare time. I thought you might enjoy seeing it. You know, because you liked these houses so much."

I barely heard him. I was wondering around the living room looking at every detail. The wooden shelves, the framed art, and even family photos. I was taking it all in while he was still talking. Then one of the pictures caught my eye.

"Hey, why is there a picture of Sal here? That's funny." I looked back at him.

"Sammy, this is..uh..this is my house." He stuttered.

"What? You're kidding me? NO WAY! Is it really?"

I couldn't believe it. He had bought one of the bungalow houses and remodeled it. He actually owned one of these great little houses on this great street! He bought the house that we had dreamed of buying together someday. Suddenly I was awkward again and a little jealous. I had a nice home, but this was my dream house or it was seven years ago anyway. We would drive down that street to go to the quiet beach and I would always talk about how it was the most perfect street in the world and he would say, "Sammy, one day I'm going to buy you one of these houses." We were just dreaming I suppose or I was anyway.

"Wow, it's really something. You have done such a great job remodeling too. Every single thing is remarkable, it really is, Kyle."

"I bought this house about a year after you left when the market was down and it just sat here empty for a long time. When I decided to move back here, I didn't want to move back in with my parents so I figured I might as well live in the house I owned. So I just worked on it over time as I could."

I didn't know what to say. I never knew what to say.

He continued, "I guess when I bought it, I hoped somehow you would be back but then I realized that you weren't coming back and maybe the time it took to fix it up helped me to heal and come to terms with the situation. I'm not still upset with you, but it is nice to see you again. I understand your reasons now," he paused,"Let me show you the upstairs."

I followed him up the stairs to a beautiful landing that faced the beach. It had floor to ceiling windows and the two in the middle were doors that opened out onto a small porch. On the porch were two wooden beach chairs with a table in between them.

"I love this," I said.

"This is a great place to have coffee in the morning because you can see the entire length of the beach in both directions and the sunrise is so great."

We turned the corner and he showed me his bedroom and bath. I was standing in Kyle Martin's bedroom. Too weird for words, but it was so nice. It had a masculine touch to it, but very simple décor. Then we walked back across the hall and he opened another door to a small room and he stepped aside for me to go in. The room was all windows on the beach side. It was empty except for a beautiful rug and a large chair and ottoman with a folded blanket across the back. It reminded me of a room in the beach house that my mother loved.

"Kyle, this is just breathtaking. Thank you for letting me see it."

"This was something that we talked about together so you were the one person that I wanted to show it to. I knew you would truly appreciate it."

"I'm so glad you did. It's just perfect!" I smiled, "except for one thing!"

"What? What's that?" He acted offended.

"You have this perfect house, and you're the only one on the street with NO Christmas tree! Are you trying to get kicked out of the neighborhood?" I teased. I had to change the subject just to give myself time to take it all in.

"Guess I haven't had much interest in decorating a Christmas tree with Sal?" he laughed.

"Well, we need to take care of that before the whole street riots against you!"

"That is pretty serious," he said, "guess we need to make another trip to that Christmas tree lot tomorrow."

"I guess we do." I smiled.

CHAPTER 13

It was almost lunchtime, so we headed back toward town and decided to grab lunch before going back to the house. I really needed to contact the office, but the day was just so great. I never hung out with friends at home, so just having someone to have lunch with was really fun. The town was so small, it seemed like you could see water and boats from any direction and the sun was so warm. There was a small hamburger place in town that was always a favorite, Riley's Burgers and Shakes.

"Can you believe this place is still here?" Kyle asked.

"From the looks of the parking lot, it's still packed and going strong!" I said, as we walked inside.

"Hey Kyle, how are you today? Who's this nice young lady you have with you?" The lady behind the counter called as we sat down in a booth nearby.

"Now, Mrs. Riley, look close. You might just know this face."

"What, who is she?" the lady said as she came out from behind the counter. She looked down at me over the top of her reading glasses.

"Hmmm..She sure is pretty, prettier than those other girls," she teased, and Kyle's face blushed red. "That blonde hair and green eyes, but I don't think...wait a minute...wait just a minute!" She started smiling.

Mrs. Riley was a little heavier and a little grayer than she used to be, but other than that, I would have known her anywhere. She sold me enough chocolate shakes to kill me over the years.

"Why, it can't be you, is it? Little Sammy? Is it really you? I haven't seen you since.." her voice trailed off.

"Yes ma'am, it's me, Sammy. We came back for a Christmas visit, my family and I. Kyle is doing some work on the old beach house for us. I see you're still making these wonderful burgers for everyone."

"Child, I guess I will be flipping burgers and scooping ice cream when I meet St. Peter at the heavenly gates!" She laughed. "It's just so good to see your face again. How's your Momma and Daddy doing?"

"My dad is here with me, but my mother passed about a year ago." I said.

"Oh, I'm so sorry to hear that sweetie. She was a good woman. She loved everybody and she loved this town, and animals, she loved animals too. Did you know she was always helping the animal shelter raise money for the animals?"

"No ma'am, I didn't know that. She did love dogs and cats so much, but I never knew she helped with the shelter. I guess I was spending all my summers on the beach. Do you know what she did there?"

"She would help them organize their fund raisers and would always donate some of her art work to be auctioned off. She was so talented too. I could never make things like her. She could take a stick from the beach and make a millionaire want to put it in his house." She said smiling.

"Thank you for those kind words. We miss her so much and being here makes me feel like she is close again." I said.

"Always thought she would live here one day. She called it her Happy Place", said Mrs. Riley.

"I think it's my Happy Place too." I smiled.

"Well, what can I get you kids to eat?" she asked.

After eating giant cheeseburgers and fries, we ordered my dad some food for lunch to go and headed out the door. The sun was warm, but the breeze off the water was cool.

"Does it ever snow here in the winter?" I asked, smiling. "Was that a dumb question?"

He laughed, "No it wasn't a dumb question, and yes, it has been known to snow a few times here at the ocean."

"Oh my goodness, wouldn't a white Christmas be something?"

"That would be something alright" he agreed, "never had one, I don't think. It would be pretty nice."

We were back at the house before you could blink and dad was quite happy with his Riley burger, fries and shake. Sal got in on the goodness too. She and dad had become big buddies. They slept in the sun on the porch, walked on the beach, then slept in front of the fireplace in the cool evening. Quite the relationship they were developing. He seemed happier and more peaceful than I had ever seen him in my entire life. Maybe mom's beach love had worn off on him after all. Maybe he felt closer to her there too.

CHAPTER 14

Kyle went to work on the kitchen ceiling and I went to call the office and see how I could catch up online. I had to do it, even though my heart just wasn't in it. Kind of like going to the dentist, you know you need to go, but it sure isn't your favorite thing to do. I just compared my chosen career to a dental appointment. That's great Sammy, just great.

I'm pretty sure my assistant, Howard, could run the entire office on his own. He knew I would be checking in today, so he had the most important account folders on his desk waiting for my questions. Dad's business partner had retired several years ago and sold his share of the business back to dad, so I was basically in charge of all the accounts with several other accountants working under me doing the actual work with the numbers for the individual businesses. This was a pretty slow time for us, just before the big tax season begins in January, but we still had clients that close out their year in December and were depending on our help.

"Hi Howard, how are things going?" I asked.

"Hello, Ms. Alexander, just great. Things are going just great!" he sounded a little too confident.

"Are you sure Howard, you sound like, well, like you're lying?"

"Ms. Alexander, I would not lie to you. You know that. How's the beach? How's Mr. Alexander doing? Getting some rest I hope." Howard sad.

"The beach is so great, and my dad is napping several times a day. Getting lots of rest. It's so pretty here Howard. I forgot how much I love coming here."

"But about business, is Carl finishing all the closing numbers for the Smithson account? Those are due by the twentieth? Also the final spreadsheets need to be sent over to the girl at the Oliver Building by the thirteenth. Could you please make sure those dates are on the appropriate calendars? I would like to have an office meeting on Wednesday afternoon at 3 o'clock. I will video chat into the main conference room. Please ask everyone to be there with any questions that they may have so we can take care of any issues."

"Yes, ma'am, you got it" Howard was taking notes.

"Ok, then, is there anything else we need to take care of today?"

"Well, there is one thing." He said slowly.

"What? What is it?" I panicked "Did I forget an account? Did we misplace some information? What Howard, what do you need?" Howard was used to me. He knew I panicked first and figured out the answer second.

"No, nothing like that. You just left with such short notice, that we didn't plan an office party or make plans for any employee gifts or anything. I usually assist you with whatever you decide, but you haven't mentioned anything and we are running out of time. Did you already take care of it?"

"Oh SHOOT, no I did not take care of anything, Howard. I totally dropped the ball. Let me talk to my Dad and I will get back to you before the meeting on Wednesday. Thanks for the reminder. "

"Yes, ma'am. Talk to you Wednesday"

How did I forget Christmas for the entire company? What was I going to do at this point? We always had a company party and gave bonuses to each employee, but in my rush to pack and leave, I didn't even make any plans for it.

"Sal, what am I going to do about this dilemma? Huh?" She got up and came over to lay her head on my lap. Her big brown eyes seemed to say "everything will be ok, don't worry."

"Want to go for a walk on the beach, Sal? Huh? Do you?" Her tail wagged in happy agreement. Maybe a great idea would float to the surface, and if not, a beach walk would make me feel better anyway.

"Hey, Sal and I are going for a walk on the beach before it gets too cold." I yelled through the door."

"Stop stealing my dog!" Kyle yelled back. "You're gonna spoil her!"

"Yep, that's the plan! Be back soon!"

Sal was so used to the beach, she didn't need a leash. She would run after a sea gull, but then she would come right back when she remembered that they could fly and she couldn't.

"Sal, do you really remember me, or do you just love everybody?" I wondered out loud. She did come running into me that first day like a friend she hadn't seen in years. Maybe she did remember, maybe she liked everybody, either way, she reminded me that the love of a good dog was a great thing to have, and that sometimes love keeps loving even after you leave.

"Do you remember my mom, Sal? She used to sneak you treats, and let you off your leash to chase birds when she wasn't supposed to. She let you sleep beside her on the big swing and didn't even care if your doggie hair got all over it." She stared at me like she completely understood and nuzzled her soft face against my hand.

"Yea, you probably remember. She was too nice for you to forget."

How could I tell those sweet brown eyes goodbye again when it came time to leave? She wouldn't understand why I was gone again. I hoped she wouldn't be sad. I knew I would be. Could I possibly stay? Sadly, I knew it would never work.

We walked a couple of miles down the beach and turned to head back. The wind was getting colder. This time of the year only gave about five hours of warm weather then it would start to cool off again in the early afternoon. As I walked, I thought about Kyle and his house. How it must have felt to buy that place after it had been a dream that we shared together. He was probably heart broken. I'm sure he didn't even tell anyone except maybe his mom, he told her most everything. He was a very handsome man, I wonder why he never married. Surely there was someone in this town he could love. Maybe for the same reasons I didn't. I dated a few times, but with work I just never had time and no one ever felt right. No one ever felt like it did with him.

I was almost back in front of the house when I looked up to see him and Dad walking toward me. My dad struggled to walk in the sand, but Kyle walked beside him patiently.

"Can't a girl get away from you two?" I teased.

"Your dad needed fresh air and I brought a Frisbee!" He waved it in the air.

"Kyle, you know that I cannot throw that darn thing!" I said.

"Sammy, you're a grown woman with a college degree. You run a huge business. Surely you can throw a Frisbee now."

He backed up about fifty feet, warned my dad to get out of my way and flung the Frisbee at me. I ran to get it, and just as I reached to grab it, Sal came out of nowhere and jumped to catch it in her mouth.

"Hey, I almost had that!" I shouted. She ran over and dropped it at my feet.

"I think she was helping you." Kyle said. "Maybe just say thank you!"

"Ha-ha, very funny! You are *veeery* funny!" I grabbed the Frisbee and got ready to throw it back. I did the throwing motion without letting go a couple of times to get ready. How hard could it be? People do this all the time, it was a Frisbee for God's sake, not brain surgery.

"You ready?" I shouted.

"Not getting any younger!" He shouted back.

"Wow, ok here goes!"

I flung it hard to make sure it would make it all the way to him. The Frisbee went up at a 45 degree angle and headed straight back at me. I screamed, jumped out of the way and it landed right in the waves. Sal went leaping into the water to retrieve it.

"Ok, well, now we know, you still can't throw a Frisbee." He winked. As he came closer, I kicked cold water on his pants. "No, you did not just do that!"

"Looks like I did just do that!" I smirked. He kicked water so hard, it wet my clothes and even my hair. It was freezing. I was screaming, Sal was barking and my dad was bent over laughing at us.

"Ok, ok I give up." I said. "It's so cold!" I took off running to the house with sopping wet Sal right on my heels, still thinking it was a game. Kyle walked with Dad, both of them enjoying a good laugh at my expense. It was so great to see my dad laugh like that again. Who am I kidding, it was great to feel myself laugh like that again.

I changed clothes while Kyle built a fire in the fireplace and dried Sal with an old towel. She curled up and went straight to sleep. The sun had gone down and I realized that dinner time had passed. We hardly had any groceries in the house, so I was searching for something to fix, and Kyle was picking up his tools and carrying things to his truck.

"Tomorrow I will start on the leaking problems in the bathroom." He said.

"That's fine," I said. "I would invite you to stay for dinner, but I honestly have no idea what we are going to have. Probably just a sandwich or something.

"I have an idea" he said, "be right back."

"Where are you going?" I yelled after him. He had already jumped in his truck and headed out of the drive. He was always like that when we were dating. If I so much as mentioned wanting something, I would turn around and he was gone to get it. In just a few minutes he was back with a couple bags from the market.

"What on earth did you get," I asked peeking into the bag.

He pulled the bag closed. "Geeze, girl, did anyone ever tell you how nosey you are?"

"Someone did a few times," I laughed.

"Just go do something, I will be finished in a few minutes."

I obediently went to the living room and started putting one of the new pillows on the sofa and turning on the Christmas tree. Whatever he was cooking, smelled heavenly.

"Ok, let's eat!" he yelled from the other room.

"What are we eating?"

His face got serious, "Several years ago, this nice lady invited me over to dinner in this very house and she made her famous clam chowder. I loved it so much that she bagged up the left overs, froze them and gave them to me the next day with a handwritten recipe. I have been making it ever since."

"Kyle, you made my mom's clam chowder? I haven't had it in years!" It made me happy just thinking about it.

He had poured the chowder into mom's pretty blue bowls and added tiny oyster crackers and cheese just like she did. It was creamy and warm and delicious. We took our bowls to the living room and sat on the sofa in front of the fire with the tree sparkling.

It was a simple dinner, a simple day, a great day like I had not had in a long time. I was beginning to understand my mom's deep love for this old house. There was a peace here, a quietness that I couldn't find in the city.

"This soup hits the spot, Kyle." Dad said. "Really good."

"Thanks John, maybe I will be a chef someday."

"Do it! If it makes you happy! That's my advice." Dad glanced at me.

I laughed, "Since when is that your life motto, Dad? I'm not sure your job made you happy at all."

"You're right, Sammy." He got serious. "I wasn't happy, but I did it anyway. Now my life is short and I don't get a do over. I should have spent more time doing something I loved, and you should too. Shouldn't she Kyle?"

Kyle looked surprised, "Umm, I think I will just mind my own business on that one. But I guess life is too short to not be happy."

"Ok, you two philosophers finished yet?" I joked. "My early morning is catching up with me."

"I know I'm finished," said Kyle, "got to get home and get some rest. Plenty to do tomorrow and then someone promised me a trip to buy a Christmas tree."

"I didn't accomplish very much around here today, so work, work, work tomorrow for me. I need to finish the living room, get the bedrooms ready, paint those chairs on the porch and buy some groceries, and I should probably plan some meals... that I can't cook. Everyone should enjoy that for Christmas.

"Maybe your sister and sister-in-law can help you with some of it" Kyle suggested.

"Maybe you could just come cook for us," Dad said, hitting Kyle on the shoulder."

"Dad, surely he has something better going for Christmas than cooking for our crazy bunch." He could not be serious.

"Something will work out, you got some time to figure it out." He answered. I'm going to head out," he walked toward the door, "I'll see you in the morning sometime."

I followed him to the porch.

"Thank you for showing me the house today." I said, "It was really nice. I'm glad you have it. It is such a great place for you to get to live."

"Yep, you're welcome. Maybe the neighbors won't kick me out if I get that tree up tomorrow. Thanks for coming."

"Ok, goodnight, Kyle."

"Goodnight, Sammy." He bent over and gave me a quick hug. It caught me completely off guard.

"Oh, sorry about that. I didn't mean to do that." He was embarrassed.

"It's fine, we're friends. It's ok. I will see you in the morning. Drive safe."

I was a grown woman. I'm not going to make too much out of a simple little hug from a friend. No big deal at all. No big deal except the person hugging was once the love of your life, the only person you had ever been in love with. Was it just being here at the shore or what? It seemed like every decision I knew was right and good was beginning to be a big question now. Was I totally wrong to leave all those years ago? Should I have never left in the first place? Being with him again felt so comfortable, so easy. I was having to work at not being comfortable. My head was spinning. At times like this, a girl really needed her mom to talk to and give her advice. I sat down on her swing and covered up with the blanket. It was still too cold, but I felt close to her here. What would she say to me right now? What would her advice be? I missed her so much more than I ever let myself admit. That's what I do, I take care of business and I don't let myself feel. But here at the shore, I feel everything. I feel close to my mom and I miss her at the same time, and I realize I missed Kyle so much more than anyone ever knew.

I was so sad for the loss in my life. The loss of my mom of course, but the loss of Kyle and what we had and what our future was supposed to be. I had lost all of that because of my decision to leave. I might never feel that way again about another person and that made me very sad. How could I have known all that so many years ago when I had to make that decision. How could I know it would feel like this? How could I know that he had a piece of my heart that I would never get back?

I didn't know how Kyle felt either. This girl, the girl he planned to spend his life with, just walked away. Then one day, she just walked back into his life, or did she. Was she just going to fix this house, celebrate Christmas and be gone again? I was sure that he didn't know how to feel, but I wasn't sure if he was feeling anything or not. Maybe I should just ask him straight out, like straight to the point. We are adults now. We can have a very adult conversation. Yea, that's not happening.

CHAPTER 15

I must have overslept because I could hear my dad and Kyle talking about the house when I woke up. He was already there? I jumped up and scrambled to get dressed, catching a look at myself in the mirror. My hair was all over the place, no makeup, morning breath and he was in the bathroom. GUM, maybe I had gum in my purse. I found a mint, pulled my hair up and threw on a baseball cap. Leftover eyeliner gave me raccoon eyes, but I fixed that quickly. I swung open the bedroom door.

"Oh, hey!" I said, casually. "Didn't know you were here."

"Gotta get this job finished soon." He said. "I have some other work to get to."

"Oh, yea, of course you do." I said.

Weird. Did that mean he didn't want to come by or what. Why should he? I would be leaving again soon. Why would anyone want to put themselves through that? Stop overthinking it, Sammy! I'm sure I was reading into it too much, besides, why did it even matter?

"Hey Dad, did you make coffee already?" I headed toward the kitchen.

"Yea, there's some left in the pot." He yelled back.

I fixed my coffee and headed to the porch with a notepad and pen. I worked better with a good list and I needed a good list. I had to finish up the house, make a decision about the office Christmas dilemma, get family gifts, and plan some sort of meal for Christmas day. I was used to running an office, but all of these things were outside my area of expertise. I also needed to touch base with Amy and see how their trip planning was going.

Kyle walked through the screened porch to go to his truck, without a word.

He was night and day different from the night before when he made dinner. Maybe it was the hug, maybe it spooked him. He started back through,

"Hey, we still going to get that tree today?" I stopped him.

"Oh, I guess, if you still want to." He answered.

"Sure I do, why wouldn't I want to?" I said. "What time were you thinking? And just curious, do you have any decorations because I'm betting that you don't."

He smiled, finally, "Well, you would win that bet because I do not have any decorations at all."

"Ok, you need a tree, and decorations and I need some more gifts for my nieces that are coming. Anywhere we can do that?"

"There is a mall about forty-five minutes away but we might have to leave earlier then come back by the tree lot." He said, "If you have time for that."

"You seem a little short on time yourself." I questioned.

"Oh, well, that, I can work it out." He looked away, knowing she had seen right through him.

"Ok, if you're sure. Just let me know when to be ready. And can you tell my dad to come out here? I have something I need to ask him?"

Dad came out to the porch, putting on his sweater and sat down on the swing.

"What is it Sammy? Kyle said you needed me for something."

"Well Dad, I talked to Howard and it seems that I forgot a pretty important detail."

"Detail? About what?" He asked.

"Well, in our rush to leave and get here, I didn't leave any instructions for a Christmas party or for Christmas gifts for the entire office. I don't know how I overlooked it. I'm sorry Dad, I really dropped the ball on that one."

I had worked with my dad long enough to know that he would not be happy with me for forgetting this. He took good care of his employees and did not like it when they were overlooked. So I had prepared myself for a big lecture.

"Oh don't be so hard on yourself, Sammy." Dad said. "Let me think about it and we will come up with something."

"Okay, who are you and where is my driven workaholic father?" I teased.

"I guess I'm just starting to realize some things that I wish I would have realized years ago. I wish I would have slowed down while I still had your mother her to enjoy life with. All those walks she wanted to take down there on the beach every day. It always looked the same to me." He sighed. "It looked the same to me because I was too busy to really see it. I saw water and sand and you kids playing sometimes, but she, she saw in vivid color, every detail. I think every time she walked down to that shore, it was like seeing it for the first time all over again."

He looked sad. More sad than I had seen him in a while, but peaceful too.

"That's kind of how I feel when I'm here too, Dad." I said.

He smiled, "Your mother would show me a sea shell she had found and to me it looked like the other seven million she had brought up to the porch, but to her it was a jewel that was completely different than any she had ever seen before. Remember after we would go to the beach and we would have been home for months and she would reach in her purse to get something and pull out a stray seashell that she had thrown in there on her way out the door of this place?" I asked laughing and blinking back tears.

"That woman could have been a junk collector!" Dad laughed. "She would see a piece of driftwood and want to make a table. Shoot, all I saw was a hunk of dead wood covered in sand. But I don't want to see with my eyes anymore, Sammy. I want to learn to see a few things like she saw them. I want to slow down and appreciate the little things."

"Time seems to naturally slow down here, doesn't it?" I said.

"It does for sure." He agreed, "So let me think about the gifts and we will handle it. Did I hear you say you were going shopping and to buy a tree?"

"Yea, Kyle showed me his house the other night and he doesn't have a tree so we are going to get one and some other presents for the girls. Do you want to come with us?"

"Yes I do, that would be great. I talked to George down at the hardware store and he told me to come by and visit with him for a while. I think I would like to catch up with an old friend. Will Sal be okay going along with you two, or she can stay here? By the way, where is his house?"

I sat there for a second, "Dad, he bought one of the bungalow houses outside of town. The ones I always loved. It's straight across from the beach. He remodeled it and it is so perfect. The porch, the trees, it's just perfect."

"Sammy, listen to your heart and not your head this time, okay?" Dad looked me straight in the eye.

"What do you mean, Dad?"

"You know what I mean, Sammy."

I knew what he meant, I just didn't know how to do it. I had closed my heart seven years ago. I realized then that it either had to be a hundred percent closed or a hundred percent open and I couldn't let myself miss him that much, so I chose closed. I didn't let anyone close to me anymore. I didn't really have friends and even my mother and I weren't as close before she passed. Funny thing about the heart, it can be so soft and caring, but it can turn so hard and cold to keep from hurting. My heart was starting to care again and it was very unfamiliar territory.

CHAPTER 16

I spent the day working on the house and checking things off my list. I wanted to make sure dad had dinner available because George was going to drop him back by the house when the store closed, but he said he was fine and could take care of himself and Sal. I never remembered him enjoying our pets. Mom was the dog lady, but he seemed to love Sal and her company and she loved having someone nap as much as she did. My dad had turned into a different person in a week. Maybe I had too. I needed to at least get my hair out from under that hat and put on some decent clothes before Kyle got back to pick me up.

I didn't exactly pack to be going out anywhere nice or to care how I looked so my wardrobe was limited to jeans, hoodies and long sleeve t-shirts, and one nice sweater. Guess I would go with the sweater. I didn't actually have a lot of clothes to wear besides professional office clothes since I didn't do very much apart from work. I had managed to make time to go to the gym and stay in shape and I had to keep my nails and hair presentable for the office so I wasn't a complete wreck. The sweater was a soft blue and I liked it with my eyes, so I was feeling pretty good by the time I heard Kyle's truck pull into the drive.

He walked up onto the porch with Sal leading the way and knocked as he opened the door.

"Come on in," Dad yelled, "Well, you clean up pretty good, don't you?"

I came down the hall just as he turned to answer. He was wearing jeans and sweater too. I had only seen him in work clothes. He had fixed his blonde hair and shaved and was wearing suede casual shoes that looked good with his jeans. He was extremely handsome, even more so than when we were younger. His face had matured and he had obviously seen the gym a day or two.

"Hey, you're all..cleaned up and fancy." I smiled.

"Well, I wasn't going to come in dirty work clothes," he laughed.

Why were we both so nervous? We had been a million places, a million times over. I felt like I was going on a first date at sixteen. Why was my stomach weird all of the sudden. And when I get nervous, I talk. Usually senseless talk, but talk nonetheless. I grabbed my list and hurried dad to the car before he could think to say anything. I scrambled out the door, like any sixteen year old before her daddy could harass her date. We drove through town and dropped dad off at the hardware store to see George.

"You have fun, honey." He said. "I will meet you back at the house later."

"You look nice," Kyle said, when dad got out of the car.

"Oh, thanks, but I didn't bring a lot of clothes for going out, so we can only go one place because I only have this one sweater." I laughed nervously, "Otherwise, I will need to wear workout clothes."

"I don't think I have ever seen you look bad in anything you have ever worn, so I will take my chances." He said.

"Ok," I laughed, "then you can't say anything when I come out with sweats and a hat for dinner."

"Deal" He agreed, "So there's a department store that maybe we can find what you need plus some tree decorations, then maybe grab some take-out and head to the house to save me from the Christmas carolers."

"Ok, sounds good to me."

The ride was nice. He pointed out new places that had popped up and old places that were still around. We chatted about his parents and how they were doing and about my sister and brother and what their lives looked like. He was very close to his parents. I wondered if they hated me for leaving him like I did.

"Hey, do your parents know I'm here?" I asked.

"No, I haven't exactly felt the urge to tell them that," he said, "my mom will worry and make my dad listen to her worries. Since she has nothing to worry about, I didn't see any reason to tell her. Besides, Sammy, all that was a long time ago. It's in the past. We are not the same people and today I need a Christmas tree!"

"True! And a Christmas tree you will have!"

His mother and I were very close, but I knew hurting him meant hurting her. But today, we were going to have fun, do some shopping and not think about the past and maybe not the future either.

The store he picked had everything we could possibly want. I had to buy toys from my dad for my brother's girls and a few things for my brother, his wife and my sister.

"Believe it or not, I already bought gifts for these kids and brought them with us." I said.

"Then why are we buying more?"

"The stranger that has overtaken my father's body insists on buying them more toys to open on Christmas morning, so they can have a big day." I said using finger quotations.

"The stranger?" He looked confused.

"Yes! My dad has turned into someone that I don't even recognize since we have been here. He is thoughtful and wants to enjoy every minute, and take walks on the beach. Yesterday I told him I forgot to plan Christmas for the office. I worried about telling him all night and he just said to not worry, we would think of something. I don't even know this person. Maybe this town is magical." I laughed.

"More toys he wants, more toys he will get!" Kyle said, as he started filling up the cart.

We laughed and played with every toy that went into the basket. I was surprised the store didn't ask us to leave. A very tall man on a pink bicycle was quite the sight. And anything that made a sound or had a button, he was touching.

"Oh my gosh, you are like a five year old!" I laughed.

"Basically yes! But these are really cool! I know they are girls, but let's get them nerf guns so they can shoot Mac. He will love it."

I laughed, "You don't know my brother anymore. He isn't as much fun as he used to be. I doubt he even plays with the girls. They keep them so busy with dance lessons and music lessons and language lessons. I don't know if they even know what a nerf gun is."

"In that case, we are definitely getting them." He said as he threw two guns into the cart. "When I have kids, they are going to play like kids, like we did. I guess music and dance is important, but what happened to playing outside and getting dirty and making mud pies. I want my kids to spend their days building sandcastles in front of my house and running through the sprinkler in the front yard, catching lightning bugs at dusk and being so tired from playing all day that I have to carry them up those stairs to bed every night."

"Wow, you've given this a lot of thought, haven't you?"

"Well maybe not a lot, but some." He looked embarrassed. "I just had so much fun growing up here in this small town. I learned to ride my bike on these sidewalks and learned to surf before I was in middle school. When I worked in the city, all of the people I worked with spent their time working to make more money just to buy their kids computers and cell phones and making sure they were in the best preschool so they would be accepted to the best college. Whatever happened to just being a kid and having some fun playing with your dad on the beach?"

"I can honestly say, that I don't really think about having kids much less where I want them to play." I said.

"You don't want kids someday?" He asked.

"I mean, yea I guess so, someday. I love kids and all, I just work so much that I don't think about that part of my life."

"Sounds like you need to take a day off and play in the sand a little bit yourself."

"Yea, I probably do."

After destroying the toy department, we moved on to the Christmas decorations. I forgot how much I loved Christmas. They had everything and I loved to decorate, so we bought wreaths, lights, ornaments and candy canes to go up the sidewalk. We loaded his truck like Santa's sleigh and headed back toward the beach.

It wasn't quite time for dinner, but we decided to stop on the way and grab Chinese food to go, then on to the tree lot. They had sold a lot of the trees but they still had several to choose from.

"Ok, you need a big fat one!" I said.

"And why is that?" He asked. "Why not tall and skinny?"

"Because fat trees have lots of room for lots of ornaments." I explained.

"Really?"

"Ok, I don't know, I just like them. Can we get a fat one please?"

"Do you have a fat one at your house?" he asked.

"My house? Oh, well, I don't actually have one at my house either, but neither do my neighbors, so I'm safe."

"Where do you live, Humbug Lane?" He laughed. "You don't have a tree, your neighbors don't have trees. Does Santa not come to that city either?"

"I'm not sure about that one, but I'm pretty sure he doesn't come to my house."

"Ok, fat it is then!" he agreed, "and we are going to need a stand or something to hold it up."

Pretty soon, we were loaded and headed to his house. The sun was starting to set as we headed through town. People were still out shopping and having coffee and dinner. I guess they all knew Kyle because everyone waved as we passed by. We turned on the pretty little street and headed to his house. I couldn't help but wonder what it would be like to live there. Yes, I had made my choice, but I could wonder, couldn't I?

"Look at that, Sammy." Kyle said, and nodded toward the water.

It was breathtaking. The sky was pink and orange and purple all painted together. The clouds had blocked part of the sun so it was shooting out around them in every direction.

"Oh my gosh, it's just so beautiful! No matter how many times you see it! Do you ever get used to seeing that?" I asked.

He laughed, "I probably don't appreciate it as much as I should or as much as you do right now, but it does still amaze me on a regular basis. Sometimes after a hard day, I take my dinner up to the upper deck and sit out there to eat. Somehow taking all this in puts things back into perspective for me. I love the mornings too though. Sometimes I can see dolphins playing and swimming up the beach early in the morning in the summer when I'm having my coffee."

"NO YOU CANNOT?" I was excited to hear that. I used to love to get up early enough to see the dolphins in the morning. I had forgotten about that part of the beach.

We pulled into the drive and walked up onto the porch. I sat down on the steps to take in the last few minutes of the daylight and Kyle plopped down beside me, almost landing on top of me. Our eyes met for one split second.

"Oops, sorry about that!" He said, sliding over.

"It's okay, you don't have to be so awkward around me. I'm not going to bite you." I teased.

"Yea, I wasn't worried about you biting me." He said with a wink.

We both looked at the water until the darkness swallowed it up and gradually the Christmas lights began to pop on down the street.

"Look! Why didn't we get one of those?" I said, pointing at the neighbor's yard.

"A giant snow globe full of Styrofoam balls? Oh, I don't know how I could have missed out on one of those." He laughed.

"I'm still crossing my fingers for a few real flakes. God knows it's cold enough!" I said. "That wind off the water is brutal."

"It is cold for sure, let's get this tree inside and get busy, besides I'm getting hungry."

"Of course you are." I laughed, "Some things never ever change."

We unloaded the truck, except for the toys and gifts. Kyle put the tree into the stand while I put dinner out on plates. We decided to eat first, then start on the tree. We chatted all through dinner. It was easy and comfortable and if I wasn't mistaken almost flirtatious. Then again, it had been awhile since I had flirted or had been flirted with so I hoped I wasn't reading it wrong.

He pulled all the lights out of the packages and began to put them around the tree.

"Ok, wait, you know this has to be done a certain way, right? That's why I wouldn't let my dad do it." I took the lights to show him.

"Well, I didn't, but as long as I have known you, I probably should have known that, yes. But since you don't even have a tree yourself, I'm not sure how you became the authority on the subject."

"I may not have a tree now, but this was my job my whole life every Christmas and some important things like this, you just don't forget. In and out of the branches, so they are all lit up nicely. Then next we hang all the balls." I explained.

"Sammy, must everything you do have an order to it?" he asked. He wasn't being mean, just asking.

"Well, no. Well, yea, most things. Okay, almost everything I do is planned. I'm so sad, aren't I? You must think I live this sad little routine life with no excitement and no veering off the plan."

"Well, do you?

"Do I what?"

"Veer off the plan. Because I don't think that at all." He said, more seriously, "I think you made a choice to follow a plan that someone else made for you because you wanted to help them and to make sure they were taken care of. But I think there is a part of you that wants to throw caution to the wind and throw that plan in the trash and see what part of life you have been missing?"

"And what if I do want to do that?" I said looking up at him.

"What if you do?" He asked back as he stepped closer, looking down at me. "What if you do and it turns out to be really great and it's not quite as scary as you think it will be? What if instead of falling, you end up flying?"

Kyle always had the uncanny ability to see right through me, and to know what I was thinking and feeling even when I couldn't quite sort it all out myself. He wasn't surprised when I had left, just hurt and disappointed. I wasn't very good at serious conversation or with talking about my feelings.

"Ok, you can put all these ornaments on the top half of the tree any way you like and I will do the bottom half." I changed the subject. My best talent.

"Hmmm, a compromise or a challenge?" he asked.

"Most definitely a compromise, but my half will look the best!"

"You're on, and you, my dear are going to see that everything doesn't have to have a plan and a pattern." He grinned slyly.

We carefully hung all the ornaments with each of us stepping back to check our work. We laughed and teased each other like old times, but we didn't really talk about the past until Kyle said, "Remember those perfect sand castles we used to build on the beach? You would draw out the plans and we would work on them for hours, but we always won that crazy contest."

"Yea, the plan was that I would draw out castles that we would build and you would do all the work to make it happen." I said without thinking. "See, having a plan made us the winners every time."

"Do you still draw all those house plans?" He asked, "You know, how you were always scribbling them down on pieces of paper when you got inspired by some door or porch?"

"Oh I remember, but no I haven't drawn anything like that in forever. I couldn't." I said.

He looked at me kind of strange, "Couldn't?"

"Kyle, I know you think I just left and went about my little life at college, but you don't understand at all. I left, but I left part of my soul here. I was heartbroken leaving you, and Sal, all our dreams and plans. I went home and packed up that part of my life. All of the things we shared, all of my drawings, all of our letters, everything we had went into a box. I closed it, taped it, and shut the door on it. That was the only way I could do what I felt like was my only choice at the time. I went to school and I studied and made good grades, but drawing or studying houses was nothing to me anymore but a sad reminder of what my life could have been but was never going to be. It was the only way I could move forward."

"So you never looked back?" he asked.

"I told myself I could never go back, so there was no reason to look back. Just keep moving forward, Sammy. Stay busy and it will get easier."

"And did it? Get easier?"

"I mean, yea, I guess time heals all wounds they say, so eventually it got better and when I got out of school I was so busy learning about the business. Then my mom found out she was sick and I was busy with that for some time. My brother and sister don't live near us, so it was only me and my parents. I just did what I had to."

"That's a pretty heavy load, Sammy." He said, "What about you?"

"What do you mean?"

"What about your life, what you need, what makes you happy?

"Don't get me wrong," I said, "I don't hate my life or anything. I don't hate my job or hate my parents for ruining my life. I have a good life. I do, really."

"Ok, are you trying to convince me or yourself?" He said laughing. "And so now that you have come back here, how's that lid on that box fitting?"

"That box and its lid" I paused, "well, let's say it's not holding together as well as it once did. This place makes me remember all those things that I learned to forget."

CHAPTER 17

We finished the tree and Kyle tried to convince me that his thrown together décor looked just as nice as my well placed decorations, but I was sure that my neatly placed ornaments were the best, probably over thought, but still the best.

Next on the agenda was to hang lights on the porch. It was freezing but we threw on jackets and he found me a sock hat and we got started. He was finishing the lights and asked me to go inside and get an extension cord from the laundry room. I ran inside and started rummaging through the cabinets and drawers. As I opened the top cabinet and saw a wooden box on the shelf and pulled it down to see if it had a cord in it.

Seems as though Kyle had a box of his own. He had every note and letter I had ever written to him. It had every scribbled drawing on every napkin that I didn't even know he had paid attention to. All of the pictures we had taken together and with Sal when we first got her, they were all there. He had saved every little thing that had connected us so many years ago. I put the box back on the shelf and grabbed the cord and headed back out to the porch, hoping he wouldn't notice my trembling hands.

I went out the door and handed him the cord.

"Here you go." I said, nervously. I wasn't sure I wanted him to know that I saw the box.

"Gosh did you get lost?" He said, taking the cord to plug it in. "I'm freezing out here."

He plugged in the lights that went all around the porch and down the banisters on the stairs.

"Whoa! It looks magical!" I gasped. "Do you like it?"

"I must say, it looks pretty fantastic!" He agreed. "Now maybe I can show my face around the neighborhood, but can we go inside now before we turn into icicles?

He reached to open the door but it was locked. He tried again harder, rattling the door knob.

"Oh no, it's locked." He said.

"What? How? I didn't lock it!"

"I guess the lock flipped over or something, I don't know. " He said, using both hands now.

"Ok, let's think, don't you have a tool or something in your truck?"

"Well, my truck is full of Christmas gifts, so I locked it and my keys are inside." He said, almost laughing.

"And this is funny, why?

"Isn't this just like something that would happen to us?" he laughed out loud.

I had to laugh too. He was right. Somehow crazy things always seemed to come our way.

"Like the time we drove to the beach and locked the keys in your truck and didn't realize it until a horrible storm blew in and we couldn't get into the truck. We just had to sit there in the pouring rain." I remembered.

"Exactly!" He said, "But it wasn't this cold. Come on, we got to break into my house!"

"This should be entertaining!"

He headed around the side of the house checking each window. They were all locked. We got to the back of the house and there was one window about eight feet off the ground.

"That window isn't locked because the lock is broken and I haven't replaced it yet. I'm going to need to boost you up there and you climb in and go unlock the front door. Okay?"

"Seriously?" I asked, surprised.

"Do you have a better idea, before we freeze?"

"Okay, okay start boosting."

"Alright, put your foot into my hand and I'm going to push you up to the window, then you push the window up and I will try to push you up so you can get inside.

"Recipe for disaster." I mumbled.

I followed his instructions, put my foot in his hand and he boosted. I went straight up the edge of the window and caught the ledge of the window sill.

"You got it?"

"Yea, I think so."

I did *NOT* have it. My hand slipped off the window sill and I fell backwards.

I screamed, but he caught me. There we were in the freezing cold, in his backyard with him holding me in his arms looking at each other, face to face. We both busted out laughing.

"Well that went well." I giggled.

"Really good for the first time." He agreed. "Let's try again, you can do it."

He sat me back down on the ground in front of him and put his hands back out in a cup for my foot to fit into.

"By the way, have you gained a couple of pounds?" He said, just as he hoisted me over his head.

"Oh no, you did not just say that! You did not just make fun of my weight as you picked me up?" I was reaching for the window again.

He was belly laughing at this point, trying to balance me on his hands. Somehow I managed to push the window up and he gave me one final shove. I was able to heave myself over the edge of the window and into the bathroom floor. I turned around to look back down at him.

"Great Job! You did it!" he yelled.

"Yes I did, and after that weight comment, I may leave you out in the cold for the rest of the night." I yelled back.

"Come on, Sammy, you know you're not an ounce bigger than you were at eighteen." He lied.

"I'm sorry, what?"

He yelled again, "you haven't gained any weight, you're so tiny, and you're still beautiful!"

"Alright, that's better! Go to the front door." I shut the window.

I ran to the front room to let him in. He busted through the door giving me a high five and a big hug that lifted me off the ground.

"Teamwork! Good Job!" he said.

He walked over to the fireplace and hit a button and the gas logs popped on.

"Now that should warm us up in a few minutes. Want some coffee or hot chocolate?" he asked.

"Kyle Martin has a cheater fireplace? I can't believe it."

"Hey, no making fun of the fireplace. It's easy and it's clean, which makes it perfect."

"Umm, no coffee, but maybe some hot chocolate. Got any marshmallows?"

"Yes I do actually. Are you going to roast them or put them in the hot chocolate?"

"In the hot chocolate, of course."

He went into the kitchen to fix the hot chocolate and I moved closer to the fire to thaw out. His living room was cozy and comfortable, but still classy. He brought the hot chocolate over and sat down on a pillow near the fireplace.

"Hey, Sammy, I have a question and I want an answer. "

"Ok, what's the question? I will try to give you an answer." I said.

"Will you really?"

"Yes, I really will try."

"How does your heart feel to be back here? Not your head and your responsibilities, but your heart?"

I started to give my standard answer, "Kyle, I have to go." He interrupted.

"You said you would answer me."

"Ok, my heart feels like I'm home when I'm here. It feels like I belong here. I feel alive and like I'm conscience of all my feelings and thoughts and not just going through the motions, but I don't know what to do about that because I don't just have the option to stay here and go with my feelings, and it's hard to feel that way, then push it all back inside when I remember this isn't my home."

"Yea, I get that. It must be hard to feel so strongly about a place but know you have to leave it again. I never felt at home when I lived in the city. I had friends and coworkers, but it never felt like home to me. That's why I came back. Even when it was hard to be here without you here, I had to come back."

"Now can I ask you a question?" I pried.

"Sure. Anything, go for it." He was always an open book.

"I was looking for the extension cord in the cabinet in the laundry room and stumbled across a box of stuff."

"Box of stuff?" He looked confused. "Drugs, oh no, you found drugs?"

I hit him, "Shut up! No! It was a box with all of our stuff in it. And I was wondering why you still had it. Why you saved it."

"Oh, that box." He paused, his face flushed, "Well, it was important to me. You were important to me. I didn't want to just throw it in the trash, so I just put it all together and kept it in a box, with no lid." He smiled.

"Ok, I get it." I smiled back.

"I didn't want to forget you and put you behind me. I mean I had to eventually to move forward, but it wasn't what I wanted to do."

"Yea, I understand." I said.

"Do you want to look at it?" He asked.

"Sure I guess so."

He went to retrieve the box and we looked at all the photos and funny things he had saved. It brought back some sweet memories for sure. We were quiet for a few minutes, just looking at the tree and drinking our cocoa.

"Thanks for making me do that." He nodded toward the tree. "It really makes it look great in here and it feels more like Christmas."

"Your house is perfection already, but yea, it does make it feel cozier." I agreed.

"Now you just need some presents."

"I have some presents, just haven't wrapped them yet. Want to help me?"

"Sure, get them out."

He went into the spare bedroom and brought out several gifts, paper, ribbon, tape and scissors. I hadn't wrapped a bunch of gifts since I used to help my mom on Christmas Eve. Somehow she managed to get everything done except for wrapping presents and that was always left for Christmas Eve. Her room looked like Santa's workshop after a tornado, but we managed to always get it all finished.

"Who are all these for?"

"My parents, a couple of friends, and Sal." He said, holding up a bone.

"Yea, that one may get opened early if you put it under the tree."

"Hey, I have to go to a party in town on Friday for the Chamber of Commerce, and I'm supposed to bring a guest. You want to come along? It will be dinner, dancing and a bunch of boring people talking about town affairs, but it could be fun."

"Wow, you really know how to make a girl want to go out." I laughed. "Sure I'll come along. If you will tell me where to buy something to wear. Remember this is my only sweater."

"You're probably going to need a dress." He said.

"A dress! Do you know how long it has been since I had on a dress?"

"Too long, I'm sure." He winked. There's a nice store in town.

Was this a date? A date with Kyle Martin? Pretty sure my mother was doing heavenly cartwheels, kind of like the flips my stomach was doing.

CHAPTER 18

We rode home chatting about the town and all of the people and how so much had stayed the same. I told him that I never even knew how my mother had helped people and volunteered at the animal shelter. I guess I was too busy hanging out at the beach to be interested in what she was doing.

"Hey, you want to visit the shelter? I'm sure some of the same people still work there. People here don't change jobs very often." He asked.

"Yea that would be cool to go by there one day, just to see it."

We got back to the house to find Dad and Sal fast asleep in their usual places in the living room. Sal woke up, but my dad barely moved when we opened the door.

"Glad we aren't armed and dangerous." Kyle laughed.

"Maybe Sal would bark or something if we were bad people."

"Sal, you ready to head home?" Sal ran over to him. "Ok, let's go, girl.

I walked him back out onto the porch.

"Today was really fun, more fun than I have had in a long, long time." I said.

"It was a pretty good day, as good days go." He teased.

I shoved him backwards. "What? It was a great day! Except for getting locked out of the house, that is."

"Oh yea, that was not the best part, but it was pretty funny watching you struggle to climb into that little window." He was laughing harder now.

"Probably because of those few pounds I have put on! Jerk!"

"Sammy, you look as great as you did the last time I saw you." He smiled sweetly.

"Ok, I forgive you." I said laughing.

"Well now I can sleep tonight." He winked. "I will see you tomorrow, I need to get this yard cleaned up while the weather is nice."

"Ok, sounds good. See you tomorrow, then."

He leaned down and gave me a hug.

"Thanks for helping with my house. It looks really nice."

He backed up and looked at me and I nodded and smiled. "See you tomorrow. Bye Sal, see you tomorrow."

He left me standing on that porch wondering how I could turn my world upside down to keep from leaving again. How could I even be thinking like this? It was so hard the last time. I couldn't do it again. I couldn't fall for him and then leave again. I felt like I was alive for the first time since I had left him. Who knows, he probably didn't even feel the same way. Why would he? I know him and he would never open up and take the chance to get his heart crushed again. I was just asking for trouble. Maybe I shouldn't go anywhere else with him and just protect both of us. Maybe I should just play it safe and not take the chance again. I hated being that person, always safe, always making the right decision. Maybe I should take a leap and see where I land, maybe he is worth it. Maybe he wouldn't even want me to do that, but maybe he would. Lots of maybes, Sammy, *lots of maybes.*

I got ready for bed, opened the bedside table and sat that mermaid back on top. Maybe I liked those mermaid dreams a little more than I had admitted. *You win again, Mom.*

CHAPTER 19

A dress? I needed a dress! Not just any old dress, but a drop dead gorgeous dress or one that made me look that way. Why was I so worried about a dress and a party where I only knew one person? I knew who could help me.

"Hey Lizzy, it's me!"

"Hey! How's it going? How's Dad? How's the house? Wait...how's Kyle?" Lizzy had plenty of questions.

"Did you know you always blast me with questions when I call you?" I said laughing.

"Sorry, about that, I'm just happy to hear from you! So what's up?"

"Well, Dad is fine, actually really good, and actually really strange. He has turned into this laid back, dog loving, take time and enjoy life kind of senior citizen. Which is totally out of character for him."

"Completely out of character." She agreed. "Why the change do you think?"

"I don't know except he says the beach and the house makes him feel closer to mom and he wishes he would have taken the time to enjoy it more like she did."

"Ooh, that is weird for Dad to say something like that. He's not dying is he?" She laughed.

"LIZZY! Don't say that!" We both busted out laughing. "And I forgot to plan anything for Christmas for the entire office and he didn't even get upset with me!

"Well, I don't know which is stranger, that you forgot something or that it didn't bother him." She teased.

"Oh hush! Now for the interesting part and the reason I called. Kyle asked me to a Christmas party and I need a dress. A great dress! What should I wear? I need your help."

"What? Wait! So you're going somewhere with Kyle? Your Kyle? Well not, *your Kyle,* but you know what I mean."

"Ok, it's a long story, but yea, he asked me to a Christmas party here in town and I said yes and now I need a dress."

"I want to hear the story, every detail, but yes I will help with a dress. What are our options?"

There was a couple of small boutiques in town and I decided to visit both of them that afternoon. I was going to try on several dresses and video chat on my phone with Lizzy so she could see them. Her sense of style had always been better than mine so I knew she could help me find the best one.

Lizzy would support me with Kyle no matter what I decided. She always had, but she really never thought I should have left. She was excited to think that I was having fun with him again, but she didn't want me to get so attached that my heart would break again when I left. I didn't want that either.

First things first, I had to catch up with my dad and make a Christmas decision before my conference call at lunch. Whatever he had decided, would not be easy to implement this late in the game and Howard would be ready to kill me for making him handle something so big with such short notice.

He was coming up from the beach as I headed out to the porch.

"Hey dad, we need to talk about the Christmas thing for the office if you have a minute."

"Sure, honey, that's fine. I already know what I would like to do." He said, matter of factly.

"You do?" I asked. "Ok, let me grab my notepad."

I went back to the porch to sit down with him and have a discussion.

"I don't think you will need all that." He said. "It's really pretty simple."

"Well I am very curious to hear what you have come up with and I will have to sort it all out to make it as simple for Howard as possible. He doesn't have a lot of time left to pull something together, plus taking care of everything with me gone."

"Ok, hear me out," He said. "I have realized that I wasted a lot of my time working that I should have spent with my family over the years and I would like to help my employees to keep from doing the same thing. We always let everyone off for Christmas Eve and Christmas Day, but half of them work most of Christmas Eve and that's a shame. So instead of having an expensive catered party and silly gifts that no one wants, I want to close the office the week of Christmas and pay everyone for those extra days off. We can do it as a gift or whatever works for the company budget, but no more working when they should be home with their family and no more wasted money on fruit cake baskets!"

"Dad, there's no way that can work!" I was shocked.

"Why not," Kyle said, walking up on the porch. "People need to slow down a little anyway."

"Don't team up on his side." I smiled. "That's the craziest idea ever. Dad, clients are depending on us to be ready on January first and some of the guys are already covered up without having the office closed for three extra days."

"Now, Sammy, instead of thinking of why it won't work, try to think of why it will work. If everyone has a mini vacation, they will be ready to work harder when they come back."

"It's true." Kyle added.

"You, Shush! He does not need any help getting what he wants."

Dad kept going, "Besides if the office is closed, we can actually enjoy Christmas without you worrying about that place all the time."

"Should I remind you that the *place* you're referring to is your business that I have spent years working to make successful?"

"No, you don't have to remind me, Sammy. That business and I already stole too many years of your life, and I don't want to keep doing that and I don't need reminding."

He looked sad all of the sudden.

"Sorry Dad, I was only teasing you."

"I know you were, but it's true." He said. "You left everything you loved to help me with that business and I should have never let you."

Kyle turned to walk off. "You know it's the truth." Dad said to him.

"Dad, you don't have to feel that way. I made my choice."

"That was not a choice that you made Sammy. I know you thought it was the best thing to do for me and your mother, but it's your turn to live now. And maybe you can learn to do that with a few days off."

"Well, I will tell Howard, and we will figure out a way to put that in the form of a gift, in a card or something and run some numbers on it."

"No need for numbers, my mind is made up. I don't care if it looks good on paper. It feels right and that's what counts."

"If you say so Dad." I said, still trying to figure out who had replaced my father.

I went back inside to see Kyle smirking on his ladder by the fireplace.

"Stop, that smiling! Did you help him think this up? It's a no win against the both of you."

He laughed and put his hands in the air, "not guilty, but it is a good idea."

"We shall see." I said, "But right now I have to go convince an office full of employees. Then I have a very important errand to run."

"Oh yea, for what?"

"Just a dress for some party a guy asked me to go to." I smiled.

"Lucky guy." He winked.

I walked away wondering if my smile was as big on the outside as it was on the inside.

CHAPTER 20

Before I could go shopping, I had to have the conference call with the office. They were all already there waiting for me to show up, which was completely out of the norm. I am the boss that shows up first, completely prepared and ready to conduct a meeting.

We had several lead accountants that work for the company and they have assistants that work under them. They were all in the meeting, ready with questions and concerns about individual clients that Howard had sent me information about during the week. I felt like I was ready to help them with any issues.

"Good morning everyone, how's it going at the office? I hope you all are doing well and aren't having any major problems while my dad and I are gone."

Howard brought up a few issues with a couple of clients, but the person over the account had already gotten the answer they needed. They really had everything running smoothly without my help.

"Wow, it's great to see you all handling things so well, maybe I could just stay at the beach a little longer!" I joked. "I hope you all are having a great Christmas season and are getting ready for the holidays with your families. I will talk to you again before Christmas, I'm sure. Thank you for all of your hard work."

"Howard, please stay on for a few minutes so that we can tie up some loose ends."

"Yes, ma'am, they are all off the line I believe." He said, "How is your trip going?"

"Really well actually, really well." I said. "So Howard, about Christmas, my dad has one strange idea for the employee gift. Don't know if you're going to love it or hate it."

"Don't know if I'm scared or excited," Howard said.

"Yea me either." I agreed. "But here goes...."

I explained the plan my dad had told me and to my surprise, Howard didn't hate it. He thought the other employees might appreciate the time to spend with their families and still get paid for it. Plus, Dad still wanted them to have some sort of Christmas bonus to enjoy. It was win-win for everyone. Howard was going to immediately start working on getting accounts to a place that they could be ready for the New Year without everyone working through Christmas. He would design a card that we could give each employee and we would do a video conference the next week to tell them. So I could check that off the list and move on to the next thing.

"Hey Dad, Howard loved the Christmas gift idea, who would have thought?" I yelled into the other room. "We will work out the details. I'm going to town to shop. Be back in a little bit."

Now for *the dress*....

CHAPTER 21

I decided to hit the little coffee and ice cream shop before the task of dress shopping. I'm used to a latte most every afternoon at the office, and that just doesn't happen on beach time. But I haven't missed it much. Most days I looked up from my desk long enough to say thank you to Howard, who was delivering my coffee to my office because I hadn't taken time to have lunch. Here at the beach, time slows down, and lunch overlooking the water is like a daily celebration.

I sat down at a small table in front of the window to finish my coffee and I could see what looked like the entire town. The little street was busy but not too crowded with people picking up gifts from the little shops, a few people riding bikes and the glorious view of the marina and all the boats. What is it about the view of the water that settles your mind and soul? All of my summers growing up, my mother always walked to town. She said the ocean breeze was therapeutic. I think I finally understood what she meant. The big town Christmas tree was in the park in front of the marina. It was covered in white lights and blue and white balls. Everything at the beach was decorated with some shade of blue. It had always been my favorite color. All the street lights had garland on them that lit up at night. Even some of the large boats were decorated. What I loved most was the speed that life seemed to move in here. People talked to each other, knew each other and enjoyed seeing one another on the street. So unusual from my city life. Dad had neighbors he had known because they lived there so long, but not where I lived. I didn't even know anyone in my complex. I didn't even have a dog to keep me company. No wonder I worked so much.

The coffee was empty, so I left for the first boutique. I promised to call Lizzy as soon as I found a few dresses that I wanted to try on. Lizzy loved shopping and I did not, but I had to find something so I was going to give it a shot. I had no idea where to start, but I went into a shop that had a pretty dress in the window. I knew I liked classic looking clothes, no big patterns or flowers. The first boutique had some beautiful clothes, but nothing besides the dress in the window caught my eye and it wasn't a favorite. On to the next place.

I walked into the next shop doubting that I would find anything, but to my surprise, they actually had some beautiful dresses that I thought might work.

I picked out a navy dress and a black with a white collar, a white with black diamond shapes and a solid maroon. Then I called Lizzy to see which ones she thought I should try on.

"Sammy! Hey! Did you find dresses? Let me see!" She was so excited.

I had hung the dresses on the wall hangers so she could see each one clearly.

"Ok these are the four I picked, which one do you like best?" I turned the phone around so she could see them.

"Wow! Sammy, seriously, you want to wear any of these? They look like dresses for an office meeting with an important client." She was not one to hide her opinion. "None of these will work for a party, not one of them!"

"Come on Lizzy!" I argued. "They aren't that bad."

The sales lady must have heard me talking in the dressing room and asked if I needed some help and if I was okay.

Lizzy heard her and yelled, "Yes, she needs help, please help her find a dress for a Christmas party!"

"Lizzy, shhh!" It was too late, the lady had heard her and wanted to know what size I needed.

I opened the door and told her my size and that I needed to get a dress for a party there in town. She looked very happy to help, and disappeared to go find something. Lizzy was laughing at my awkwardness and I was wishing I had never agreed to this. She came back in a few minutes with several dresses to try on. I hung them up for Lizzy to see and I had to admit, they were pretty, but maybe a little too pretty for my style.

"Now those are party dresses!" Lizzy exclaimed, "Try on the red one!"

"Red! Are you sure? I'm not sure red is my color!" I argued.

"Try it on, Sammy!" She demanded

"Okay! Okay, I will try it but I'm not promising anything. Can I try the black one first?"

"Okay, but you're trying on the red one too."

I slipped on the black dress with sequins around the neck. It was fitted and made me look very slim. It was super sparkly, but I had to admit that it looked pretty good. I turned the phone around for Lizzy to see.

"That is definitely better! You have to admit, you look pretty dang hot and you know it." She smiled. "Try on the next one."

"Kinda hot, maybe." I laughed. "I'm going to try this maroon, glittery one, okay?"

It was a deep wine with gold sparkles in the fabric. It had gold around the neck and was fitted, then flared at the bottom. I liked the way it felt, comfortable, but dressy.

"I'm feeling pretty sassy in this one, Lizzy. What do you think?" I turned the phone camera.

"Ooh, Sassy Sammy! That's what Kyle will be saying."

I think my face turned the same color as the dress. I actually felt confident and pretty.

"I do really like this one, I feel pretty in it." I said.

"Well, you should, cause it looks fantastic!" She agreed. "Maybe you should think about wearing something besides sweat pants and work clothes! Now try on the red one!"

"Okay, I will." The other two made me feel a little better about the red one.

It was plain red satin, fitted to the waist with a gathered skirt that made it fluff out. It was a party dress for sure. I zipped it up and turned toward the mirror. It fit like it was made for me. Not too short or too long, but very classy.

"You ready?" I asked.

"Ready!" She said, as I turned the phone around.

"Oh My Gosh! Sammy! Is that you? Was this dress made for you specifically?"

I turned around and around looking at myself in the mirror. Lizzy was right, it fit perfectly and it looked stunning.

"Do you think it's too much for a small party like this?" I asked, "I really do think it looks pretty, but I don't want to be overdressed either."

"It's a Christmas party and your dress is red and Christmassy." She laughed. "Is that actually a word? I don't know, but you look so gorgeous, who even cares if it's too dressy or not dressy enough. Just step out and do what makes you feel good for once, and don't do it timidly. If you're going to wear a red party dress, you have to own it and do it with confidence. Now buy that dress, and go find some pretty pumps, and someone to do your nails and makeup."

"Geeze, this just got intense!" I laughed. "Ok I'm getting the dress and I will think about makeup and nails. I love you and I will send you a picture when I get all ready. Hurry up and get here would you?"

"Yes, send me a picture and I will see you soon. You're going to look beautiful, Sammy. I love you! And Sammy?"

"Yea?" I stopped to look at the phone.

"Have fun and follow your heart."

"Yea, I keep hearing that. I love you too, Bye."

The lady at the store helped me find tall black pumps that I would never be able to walk in and some pearl earrings and bracelet that matched.

"Can I help you find anything else?" She asked.

"No, I think that's all." I said, but then I saw this great sweater with a pair of jeans and those short booties everyone was wearing. "Just a minute, let me look at one more thing."
The sweater had fringe on the front, so not my style, but I was still feeling pretty confident from that red dress. I found two other sweaters, two pairs of jeans and some leggings and those booties and a scarf. I bought them all and some other earrings too. I had no idea what had gotten into me, but if I needed to look nice again, I couldn't wear that same blue sweater, *now could I*?

CHAPTER 22

The afternoon had gotten away from me and I had plenty left to do at the house. I grabbed some food and some tape and wrapping paper and headed home. I didn't know if Kyle would be there, but I got enough food just in case. We had seen each other every day since he had started working on the house. He didn't seem to mind and I had come to expect it. I didn't want to hurt him again, but I had missed this part of my life so much more than I ever realized. I was looking forward to the party and looking forward to that dress.

Kyle was still at the house when I pulled in. I could hear Sal barking from inside while I was trying to get everything out of the car. Kyle came out onto the porch.

"Do you need some help? You must have bought every dress in the town as long as you were gone." He laughed.

"Nope, I bought one dress. One very pretty dress that you will not see yet! And I bought a couple more outfits, and some wrapping paper for all those presents. I also bought you dinner, Mister!"

"Dinner? You didn't have to do that." He said politely.

"Yes, I did."

"You did? Why?" He looked confused.

"Because it was the least I could do for you helping me wrap all the presents we bought yesterday!" I threw the rolls of paper at him.

"Oh a bribe then? And I thought you were just being nice. Should've known better." He winked.

"Yea, you really should have." I laughed. "Can you carry something?"

We got everything unloaded and I set up the food for dinner, which was basically wonderful hamburgers, fries and shakes. Not a great plan for that new dress.

"Where you been all afternoon, Sammy?" Dad asked. "Thought you went out to sea and got lost."

"No sir, I did not go out to sea. I went to the coffee shop and had a latte and watched the boats at the marina. Then I went to a boutique and did a little shopping for a dress and a few other things."

"A dress? Did somebody die?" he teased, which was very entertaining to Kyle.

"Nope, no deaths. We are going to a Christmas party Friday night and I needed something to wear besides sweat pants and running shoes. So I got a dress, a very pretty dress. And you better clean up good, mister." I said, looking at Kyle.

"Well, well, a party huh? Dad said, looking at us over his glasses, like we were fifteen. "Kyle, you better be a gentleman."

"Dad! That is so not necessary!"

"Always," Kyle laughed.

We finished dinner and pulled out all the gifts and started wrapping them up. I wrapped, Kyle stuck on bows and tags and Dad wrote on the labels. We stacked them all under the tree and out into the floor.

"This looks so awesome. The girls will be so excited when they see all this stuff. They have never been to the beach either."

"Never?" Kyle was surprised. "Your brother and his wife, what's her name, Amy? Didn't they meet here at this beach? Can't believe they never came back or brought their kids back."

"Probably my fault," Dad said. "When he didn't want to take over my business, I said things that pushed him away. Me and my big mouth, making that office more important than my family again. Our relationship has never been the same since."

He looked sad. I had never seen him even think he had done anything wrong where my brother was concerned.

I interrupted, "Hey what's the Christmas Carnival thing all about? I want to take the girls while they are here, maybe on Christmas Eve."

"Oh it's great," Kyle said. "Pretty much the entire town turns out to participate and it only lasts a couple of days. They have huge slides and rides and food trucks and craft stands. Everything is all lit up with Christmas lights."

"You seem pretty excited yourself." I laughed.

"It is pretty fun and well, there's all sorts of food and dessert, so, yea, I'm in."

"Sounds like a plan for sure!" Dad said.

"So let's see the dress," Kyle said, casually.

"Not on your life! You will see the dress Friday night. "

He winked at my dad, who was enjoying the show.

"What was in all the other bags? You had an armload of stuff."

"Did anyone ever tell you that you're nosey?" I asked.

"Seems like I have heard that before, but I'm okay with it. What's in the other bags?"

"Two sweaters, two pairs of jeans, a pair of shoes and some earrings! Happy? I thought I might need something to wear besides the same blue sweater I brought."

"You bought new clothes?" Dad acted surprised and Kyle was laughing again.

"Oh my goodness, you two are impossible! A girl can buy new clothes without being interrogated, can't she?"

"We're just teasing you, Sammy, you go shopping whenever you like. In fact, you should go more often and enjoy yourself." Dad said.

"It wasn't a big deal, just felt like getting something new to wear."

"Okay, well if we are all finished here, Sal and I are going to head to the house and get some rest." Kyle stood up to go.

I followed him to the door and told Sal goodnight. He turned and gave me a hug. I hugged him back, like it was our normal routine. Why was it so easy with him, it just felt like instinct to be myself, to be comfortable, to be here?

"Bright and early tomorrow, lots to do." And he went out the door.

CHAPTER 23

I woke up the next morning to a cold rain. I loved it when it rained at the beach. Everything looked like different shades of blue grey. The waves were bigger and crashed on the beach with a tall spray, and I knew it would be pretty much empty. I needed a big coffee and a warm jacket. The sun was just breaking through the clouds as I headed out to the porch. I saw headlights pulling in and was surprised to see that it was Kyle. He said bright and early, but I didn't know he meant at sunrise.

"What on earth are you doing here so early?"

"Told you, bright and early. I want to finish up the upper bathroom and when the rain stops, I need to clean out of the gutters. What are you doing heading out so early?" He asked.

"I wanted to go for a long walk as the sun was coming up. The waves are huge from the storm too. I love it like this. Want to come along?"

"Sure, but I'm going to need more coffee, got anymore made in there?"

"Help yourself."

We headed out through the wet sand toward the beach with Sal. There was no one in either direction. The wind was blowing so hard and I was thankful for my big jacket. Sal ran to chase the two birds that were in front of us. The sky was grey, but the sun was trying to break through so the clouds were slightly pink. It was so beautiful, I had to just stop and breathe.

Kyle was watching me take it all in.

"You never stopped loving this place did you?" He asked. "You just love every little grain of sand."

"Well, maybe not every grain of sand, but I do love it. It's so beautiful, but it's more than that, it's like, all these years, going to school and work every day, I was fine and okay with my life. Now that I'm here, I found a piece of me that was missing that I didn't know was missing. I guess that sounds crazy, huh?"

"Not to me." He said. "Remember, I left for a while too. I liked my job and my apartment and the people I worked with, but in the evening when the sun would go down and I was alone, it just felt empty, like something was missing. Then when I would come home to visit, I felt full again."

"Exactly. So you just quit your job and moved back?"

"No, not really that fast or easy. I had commitments with my company that I had to complete and I had a lease on an apartment, but I just started working toward making it happen and one day I was back here trying to start a remodel on an old beach bungalow." He smiled.

"I don't know how I could ever make that happen, but it makes me sad to think about leaving that part of myself here again and going back to my everyday life."

"I guess you've just got to figure out what's best for you, not your dad, or your brother or anyone, just you. What brings you happiness and peace in your life? Where do you feel full and not empty, not just going through the motions?"

I didn't even know how to think like that and that had always been alright, but now it seemed like there was a little part of me that had been dead and was alive now. It was begging me to please do something to keep it alive and I didn't know where to begin.

"I think sometimes you have to just take a chance on something, on yourself. You know, like take a leap of faith, trust that you're going in the right direction." Kyle said.

"Yea, my mom always used to say sometimes you just got to jump and God will catch you. But you're speaking a different language to this planning girl." I laughed, but I knew he was right. "Maybe just recognizing that something has been missing is my first step. You think?"

"I'm no life coach, but I think that definitely helps."

"Hey Sammy?" He stopped walking and was looking out at the ocean.

"Yeah?"

"Sammy, I want you to be happy. I was mad before, but I was young and hurt with you. But now I just want you to be happy. If that life makes you happy and you love it, then after Christmas, I will tell you so long and maybe I will see you again someday, but Sammy, if it doesn't make you happy, then don't keep living it. Your mom has passed and your Dad is finally realizing that life is too short. There aren't any "do overs", you only get one. Please do what makes you happy. I won't lie, I never thought I would see you again and when I walked up and saw you on the beach, I thought I was seeing a ghost, but after spending time with you, I realized part of me has been missing too."

"Kyle, I don't want..." I started to interrupt.

"I know, you don't want to hurt me again. Sammy, I'm a grown man, responsible for my own heart and feelings. The only thing that will hurt me is to see you move forward in a life that you aren't happy with. Whatever you decide, I will be on your side."

"Of course you will, you always have been. You know, one of the hardest things about leaving you was that you were my best friend and I didn't have anyone to talk to about what I was going through."

"You missed me didn't you? Admit it!" He teased, kicking sand on my shoes.

I laughed, "More than I will ever admit."

He turned and hugged me tight until I hugged him back. "You're going to figure it all out, my Sammy. I know you will."

Standing on that beach wrapped in his arms, with the wind blowing the sea spray across my face, I knew he was right. In that place, at that moment, everything was right again, and there was nothing left to figure out, nothing else mattered.

CHAPTER 24

We got back to the house just as Dad had finished cooking breakfast. The house smelled like eggs and bacon and sausage. He was really a different person here. I hoped my brother could see that and they could somehow fix their relationship.

"Dad! It smells delicious in here and I'm starving and cold!" I said. Kyle started to build a fire in the fireplace.

"You're old dad can't cook too much, but I can make some breakfast. Dig in!"

We ate and laughed and had too many cups of coffee. Kyle said he had to get busy as much as he enjoyed our company. I had a job to do today that I didn't really look forward to, but it had to be done.

The beach house had a tiny bedroom on the top floor that was considered the Owner's Closet. We kept it padlocked, and guest weren't allowed to use it. When we would go home from the shore, we would store our personal items in there that we didn't want renters to use, but when we were here for weeks at a time, it was my mother's make-shift art studio. She did a little bit of everything up there. I loved the room in the summer. It had large windows on two sides and was filled with natural light. She kept white linen drapes up that she would close if the sun got too hot, but it never blocked the light. She would paint up there, or write, or just work on some project. We would wander up there with something heavy on our hearts and slip into her big chair and talk while she pretended to stay busy. She loved us fiercely so sometimes her answers were hard to take, but in the end, she somehow knew how to tell us that everything would turn out okay. It was her room, and when we left for the last time we locked the door and we never came back. I had cleaned out her stuff at home like clothes and shoes and we split her jewelry among us, but this room was her heart. I wasn't sure I was ready, but it had to be done.

I opened the lock and pulled it off the door. Even on the cloudy day, the light streamed into the room. The curtains were thin and worn, but still hung gracefully from the rods at the ceiling. Our old surf boards were crammed in front of the door. It made me smile because I knew that task was assigned to one of us teenagers and so we crammed them in and pulled the door shut. I pulled them out into the hallway. It was so cool to see them again. My brother loved to surf and was so good at it. After removing the surf boards, a cooler, a stack of beach chairs, hats and an umbrella, I could finally move around the room.

I couldn't believe it. Her easel stood there with paper on it and a watercolor painting that she had left behind. It was of one of the birds on the beach scurrying to get away from a wave. She was really very good, although she never thought so. I could almost feel her looking out that window at us at the beach. There were all sorts of shells and beads and jewelry pieces. I guess she didn't care if she finished them because she just picked up where she left off when she came back. All of her brushes stood clean in a mason jar that had paint drips down the sides. I sat down on her stool just to take it all in. Tears began to roll down my cheeks, but not sad tears, happy tears because I had found her secret.

This room was where my mother would go to gather her thoughts, to find herself and her strength. She said that it made her feel happy and thankful to be alive when she was up there painting. It gave her perspective about the rest of her life. I was too young to understand then, but now I knew. Her favorite books were here on the table covered in dust. I sat down in her arm chair in the quiet. I could hear the waves from here. I just took it all in. The stack of drift wood in the corner for some future project she had in mind, sketches of birds and dogs on the beach, and more seashells than I think was legal for any one person to pick up. The room was a pale sky blue which made it feel even more like you were outside.

I reached for one of the books and realized it was a journal. Would it be wrong for me to read it? It was her personal journal, her thoughts, hidden from everyone all this time. I opened the book slowly and knocked the dust off the cover. The first page talked about us arriving at the beach and how she was so glad that dad got to come down for the week. It was written the last summer we were here.

"Sammy, what you doing up here?" Dad called from the stairs.

I tucked the journal into a basket. I would have to get back to that later. My dad stepped into the doorway. His face lit up with a smile.

"Boy, she sure loved this room and all this stuff." He said as he ran his fingers up the paint brushes. "It's like she just left it yesterday."

I stood up and put my hand through his arm.

"I can feel her, just like she was here and has gone downstairs to make dinner." I said. "But it feels good, not sad." I smiled.

"Yea, it does," He agreed.

"Sammy, you know I bought this house as a gift for your mother. We were going to retire here together and she would finally get to walk on the beach every day. I just don't know if I can stand to put a For Sale sign in the yard."

"I can't stand the thought of it belonging to someone else either, Dad."

"Do you think I could just live here full time, Sammy?" Dad looked at me like a child asking permission for something. I didn't have the heart to say no.

"I don't know Dad, I mean, I would hate you being so far away by yourself, but I guess we could toss the idea around."

"That would be good, Sammy, thank you. I'm going to go back downstairs, maybe take a walk if the rain has stopped.

"Ok, dad. Be careful, and it's cold out there."

I didn't want to touch a single thing. I wanted to leave it just like she left it, but I knew I couldn't do that. I started picking up jewelry pieces and small shells and putting them in plastic bins. I looked thru the watercolor tablet at the paintings that were left. They were so beautiful. As I flipped, I saw a painting of a puppy, it was Sal! My mom loved her and Kyle. It gave me a great idea.

"Hey, you okay up here?" Kyle asked as he came up the stairs. I flipped the pad back over and went back to the shells.

"I think so," I answered, "it's actually quite nice. She loved it here so much. Even more than me I think."

He smiled, "Your mom was one great lady. Always doing something for someone and always cooking so much food. She sure fed me more than once."

"I think she thought it was her mission to make sure no teenager was every hungry at our house." I laughed.

"This room is just the same, like stepping back in time. Have you been crying? Are you okay?"

"Yes and yes. I was crying a little, but it was because I realized this place is where she found the strength to do all the other things that she did. It was an eye opening moment for me. Oh and my dad wants to live here now, so there's that."

"Really, that's not like him is it? I mean your mom loved it, but he always had to work and was back and forth."

"He said he can't imagine selling the house and wants to live here full time. I didn't have the heart to say no."

"Ouch, that's tough, but maybe you don't have to. He is in pretty good health and I could check on him. Maybe he could stay here just part of the year."

"I don't know, it's so much upkeep and he can't even take care of the place he lives now. I have to go by there almost every day now. But I told him we would talk about it."

"You're going to figure it all out, Sammy. You will." He took my hand. "Maybe spend some time up here and it will all come to you."

How did he do that? He always knew just what I needed. Never pressuring me, just reassuring me that I had the answer, I just needed to take the time to let it float to the surface. People say that our parents become the voices in our heads. Boy isn't that the truth. My mother used to tell me, "Sammy, if you're not sure, don't make a move, the answer will float to the surface if you give it time." Hopefully this one would float up soon. I wasn't sure what I wanted to happen to this room, but I was sure that I wanted to spend more time up there. I figured I could take the old surf boards to the thrift store or something since we didn't use them anymore, but I had an idea for one of them. The rest of the room would have to wait for me.

CHAPTER 25

"Hey Kyle, can you help me with something?"

He trotted back up the stairs, "sure, what do you need?"

"I was thinking about throwing out these old surf boards, but then I thought that one of them might make a cool shelf in one of the bedrooms."

"Sammy, are you decorating? Revamping old things into new ones?"

"Maybe a little bit, but they are just so cool." I pleaded.

"Alright, let's do this. We need to find some brackets to mount it to the wall. Where do you want it mounted?"

I cleaned it up and we put it in the downstairs room that I was sleeping in above the head of the bed. He took the bottom fin off and I added a small plant and some books on top of it. I was right, it looked awesome!

"Pretty cool," Kyle said. "I might take the other one for my house if you're just going to haul it off."

"I would rather you have it than some stranger."

"Ok, I have a little decorating idea of my own."

"Wait, what is it?" I asked. He walked away.

"Now who's being nosy?" He smiled. "Back to work for me?"

I made my way back up the stairs to get the painting tablet and the journal without my dad noticing. I wanted to read the journal, then I would tell him about it and I had some plans for the paintings. I spent the rest of the day working around the house. The sun came out, so I helped Kyle in the yard with hedges and broken limbs. I tried to stay busy, but I couldn't keep my mind off that journal. My mother passed over a year ago, and reading that would almost be like hearing her voice again. The sun came and went and Kyle headed home to get some rest. He wasn't planning to work on our house tomorrow, but said he would pick me up at six thirty and we would have dinner at the party. I was excited for him to see my dress.

I convinced Dad to turn in early so I could go to my room. Would he be hurt if I read the journal before he did? She was my mother, but she was his wife. I had waited all day and now I was second guessing myself. I took the journal from under my pillow. Just knowing it was hers made me happy to hold it. I really did experience everything in detail here. I took the journal down the hall and knocked on Dad's door.

"Dad, are you asleep?" I whispered, not sure why.

"No, honey, come on in." I opened the door slowly. I hadn't been in my parent's room late at night since I was a kid.

"Is everything okay?"

"Yea, I'm okay, but I found this today in moms art room." I held out the journal. He took it from me to see what it was.

"I wanted to read it, just to, you know, be close to her, but then I felt bad, like I was snooping in personal business. I thought you should have it. I'm sorry Dad, I just miss her so much." I burst into tears and he wrapped me up in his arms like I was his little girl again.

"Of course you do, sweetheart. I understand why you wanted to read it and it's perfectly fine. Your mother and I talked about everything, I'm sure there are no big surprises for me in there." He smiled.

"I know Dad, I just didn't want to overstep, but I could almost feel her with me again seeing all of her stuff in that room she loved."

"Tell you what," He said, "let's read it together."

"Ok, I would like that a lot." I said.

I sat cross legged on his bed and we took turns reading pages of my mother's journal. We were wiping tears and laughing at the same time. She wrote about what was happening at the time on our beach trip, about Mac meeting Amy, and me and Kyle. She wondered if we had met our future spouses. Almost in the middle of the book, Dad stopped reading.

"What is it Dad? What does it say?"

"It looks like letters to you and Mac and Lizzy from your mother." He said.

"She wrote us each a letter, all those years ago?" I couldn't imagine what it would be about.

"You should read it by yourself, Sammy. It's very special. Then if you want to share it with me you can, if not I will completely understand."

"Ok, if you think so,"

He said he was very tired and that I could take it to my room to read in private. I kissed him on the head and went back down the hall. A letter from my mom that I had never read. That was crazy, but I couldn't wait to read it.

I washed my face and got ready for bed. I turned on the light on the bedside table and took out the letter. What would she have taken the time to write down in a letter so long ago? We had a great relationship and talked about most everything, until I chose to go off to school that year. I pretty much shut everyone out at that point and just did what I needed to do. I opened the letter slowly.

The ink had faded over the years, but it was in her lovely handwriting.

My Sammy,

You will probably never read this letter, but I'm writing it to empty my heart of these thoughts, not necessarily for your reading pleasure. The summer is almost over and I have watched you make so many changes this year. I watched you meet Kyle, the love of your life. Sammy, most women live their whole lives and never get looked at the way that boy looks at you. You will be an old lady like your momma and I bet he will still be looking at you like that if you keep him around.

You are so torn, Sammy. Torn between pleasing your dad and me and helping us with the business and marrying your soul mate. I get it, we all make compromises in our lives. Some work out well and some turn out to be big regrets. I wish you didn't feel responsible for us because this may be a big regret for you. I would love for you to see that things will work out just fine, even if you choose to follow your dreams instead of taking care of mine and your father's. It's noble for sure, but I would much rather see you happy and in love and having my grandchildren.

You are probably most like me Sammy, so I know you will always come back to the shore. This summer has been so wonderful spending time together making things and painting. I hope you never lose your love for those things. You are creative, but creativity and planning don't always make the best of friends. I'm sure you will find a balance. Kyle may just be that balance. I don't know how your summer will end, Sammy, but I sure hope it ends with you choosing the shore, and Kyle and Puppy Sal. I have never seen you so happy. Dad and I will be just fine, you will see...just fine.

I couldn't even see through the tears to make it to the end. It was like sitting on the sofa beside her, listening to her advice. She knew I wouldn't be happy if I ever left here. She knew my heart belonged here at the shore, but I didn't choose that and I didn't know if I could choose it at this point. Like she always said, you don't get a do-over. I wonder if she planned to ever give me that letter. I sure could have used it a few years back, but I'm not sure she could have talked me into changing my mind. I had in my head what I was supposed to do, so I did it.

CHAPTER 26

I fell asleep thinking of her and the letter and woke up to the sun streaming through my windows. It was a gorgeous day and I needed my walk. Dad wasn't awake yet and the house was quiet. I got my coffee and jacket and headed for the sand.

Brrrr...it was freezing, colder than it had been since we got there. The sky was bright blue and the sun was blinding. The waves were calm and the water was clear, but I didn't dare get close enough to get wet. I knew it would be like ice. There was barely anyone out walking, only a few people way down the beach.

I made my way down the stretch of white sand mostly looking down at the sand because of the sun reflecting off the water. There were shells everywhere, mostly broken ones.

"Mom, you would really love this today." I mumbled. She could spot a perfect seashell before anyone else. I only found broken ones usually. I looked down and couldn't believe it. It was a beautiful pink conch shell, unbroken. It wasn't huge but it was perfect. I had never even seen a shell so pretty on this beach. It was like it was put there especially for me. Thanks Mom, I knew she was looking out for me. It was strange experiencing such details with my feelings all of the sudden, but it was real and alive too.

I headed back toward the house, but had walked further than I realized. By the time I got back, Dad was up having his coffee and poking at a small fire he had started.

"Mornin' honey," He said as I came through the door. "How's the beach?"

I stepped in front of the fireplace, "FREEZING! I keep asking Kyle if it ever snows here. I guess the air feels colder because of the water, but I would love to see it snow on the beach. Hey, look at this shell I found, it's perfect. Mom would have loved it wouldn't she?"

"That's a beauty alright." He agreed, "She loved those seashells of hers. I was always finding them in the car months, after we would get home."

"Dad, I read the letter. Would you like to read it? You can if you want."

"Sure I would love to read it, if you want me to, honey."

I went to my room and got the journal and handed it to him. He slowly read the letter wiping an occasional tear that escaped down his cheek. He finished and looked up at me over his glasses.

"I wish she would have given you this letter a long time ago before you ever made the decision to run the business. Things would have been a lot different. You would have a life with someone instead of stuck visiting your old dad every night."

"Wow that really makes my life sound horrible!" I laughed. "Dad, I made my choice and that was years ago. There's no reason to rehash it all again."

"What about now?" he asked.

"What about it?

"Sammy, I may be an old man, but I'm not too old to see how that boy still looks at you and I'm not too old to see how you look back. So I'm just going to ask... Are you going to do the same thing again?"

"It's hard Dad, I don't know what to do. I feel like I should just stay away from him and let him alone. But it's so nice seeing him again and having fun with someone. I forgot how great it is. I don't know what to do."

"Sammy, I have given this a lot of thought and I don't want you to be chained to that business anymore. Now I don't know what that looks like yet, but I'm going to find a way to get you out of there before you turn into a rock sitting at that desk."

Dad, that's my job. I can't just leave. Besides I have worked really hard to get that business where it is. I have no idea what I would do, if I didn't do that." I argued.

"Live here with me," he laughed.

"Oh so you're living here for sure now, are you?"

"I want to be here. I want to wake up to the waves every day. It's where we were supposed to be together and it's where I'm supposed to be now." He was serious.

"It's high time that you started following some plans of your own and not some list on a legal pad." He said.

"I don't know what that looks like anymore, Dad." I said.

"Lord, girl when did you get so old?" He teased. "You start by putting on that pretty dress tonight and making that boy stop in his tracks. You let down your guard, throw your legal pad away and have some fun. Stop worrying about tomorrow and next week and the business and act like a beautiful young woman at a party with a guy she has a really good time with. Would you promise me that you would just try to do that Sammy?"

"I promise, Dad, I will try."

CHAPTER 27

I made a quick run to the store for nail polish, bobby pins and some new makeup before I started getting ready. Totally not like me, but I did want to look nice and no reason to waste a perfectly stunning dress by having a bad manicure. I was nervous like a teenager going to prom and I honestly didn't even know how Kyle thought about tonight. He probably just needed someone to go with him to this boring party so he asked me to go. I'm sure he wasn't thinking anything about it being some special evening, was he?

I was putting the finishing touches on my make-up when I saw him pull in. He opened the door while he was still knocking and I heard Sal run into greet Dad.

"Hello there, Sally girl," I heard Dad say.

I had left my long blonde hair down and curled it into soft curls and had taken extra time on every detail of my makeup. I took one more quick look in the mirror and headed down the hall. They turned toward me when they heard me coming.

"Sammy, you look so pretty," Dad said. Kyle just stood there staring.

He was wearing a suit. I wasn't sure I had ever even seen him in a suit but he looked so handsome.

"Thanks Dad," I said, still looking at Kyle. "Well, does this look okay?"

"Umm, Uh...you look, umm," He cleared his throat, "you look beautiful, Sammy."

"Thank you very much!" My smile said it all.

I kissed Dad and Kyle helped me with my coat and we were on our way. The night was gorgeous. The city was lit up with Christmas lights all over it. The party was at a huge house that sat right on the beach. It was breath taking and was completely decorated for Christmas.

"Whose house is this?"

"Oh, it's the Mayor's beach house. Nice huh?"

"I'll say...it's beautiful! And why are you invited to this?"

"I did some work on some old buildings in town, so I guess they felt like they should let me come." He smiled. "Come on, let's have some fun."

The valet parked his truck and we walked into the party. Every detail was planned and so pretty. There were Christmas trees everywhere and lights and giant Christmas balls. I had never been to anything so fancy. It was a little bit intimidating. Everyone seemed to know Kyle, so he introduced me as his friend. A waiter showed us to our table in the front of the room by the dance floor and they began to serve dinner. I could barely eat for people stopping at our table to tell him hello.

"Wow, you're a very popular guy tonight." I said.

"Nah, they all just want to be introduced to you is all." He winked.

"You're sweet, but I don't know about that."

"Are you kidding? Have you seen you?" He teased. "You look stunning, and that dress is unbelievable. I mean you always look great, but you look especially great."

I smiled, "You don't look too bad yourself. Don't think I have ever even seen you in a suit, have I?"

"Probably not," He laughed, "it's a grown up thing."

"Well, we are both grown-ups, so I guess it's okay." He didn't realize that I might look like a grown up but I felt like a teenager on a first date. I literally had butterflies in my stomach. Also, I could not figure out why so many people were going out of their way to talk to him.

We were almost finished with dinner when someone got up to speak about the town and how it was growing and changing. They had some improvement projects of some sort going on. I wasn't paying close attention honestly. I was looking at all the décor of the beautiful home. When the person finished, they introduced the mayor and thanked him and his wife for opening up their home. Then the mayor got up to speak. He thanked different groups for things they had contributed to the town over the past year. Then he had an award for someone.

"This award is given this year to someone who really loves this town. They have lived here most of their life and this past year they worked so hard to make these improvements possible. They headed up the renovation project of Main Street and the restoration of the old homes and businesses there. It has been a busy year in our little town. We have visitors all year long and we strive to keep it beautiful. I am proud to give this Award to a well deserving man among us. He has given his time and talents freely and we all get to reap the benefits of that. "

"Wow, someone has worked hard." I whispered to Kyle.

"Yea, looks like it." He said.

The mayor continued, "I am proud to present this award to Kyle Martin. Come on up here Kyle!"

What on earth, that entire speech, the award, it was all for Kyle? He stood up to walk toward the Mayor and the room erupted in applause. Then everyone stood up, clapping. I stood up, but I was still amazed at what was happening. Kyle took the award and everyone got quiet and sat down to hear him speak.

"Thank you all for this great award. I'm not sure I deserve it because a project this big took the entire town to complete. I was so pleased to get to restore some of the old homes and historical sites in the town. I hope the restoration will last for years to come. I also hope that this will open doors to boost our economy and help our little town to become greater than it already is. I am honored to live in a place with such fine neighbors. Thank you."

He walked down from the podium and the people stood to clap again. I was clapping and smiling when he got back to our seats. He just looked at me with a smile and a wink.

The first man stepped back to the microphone and said, "Thank you all for your donations to the town Christmas fund, we have bought so many toys to donate to the hospital this year. Now, enjoy your dinner and dancing and have a very Merry Christmas!"

The band began to play and people headed to the dance floor. Several of them stopped to shake hands with Kyle or pat him on the back.

He finally turned to me.

"What on earth just happened?" I asked.

"Oh, nothing really, just a little award. I helped with the planning and restoration of part of the town. It was actually fun, no big deal really." He said.

"Sure looks like a big deal." I said, looking around. "Why didn't you tell me you were getting some great award?"

"It's not a big deal and if I told you, you might not have come and then that dress would still be hanging in some store. What a shame that would have been, now wouldn't it? Come on, let's dance."

Before I knew it, I was in his arms dancing. He was really good too, much better than me. It was so much fun, more fun than I had had in a really, really long time. A slow song began to play and he pulled me closer. My heart was racing.

"It's been a long time, Sammy. I missed you." He whispered.

"I missed you too." I said.

There, I admitted it. I had missed him terribly. There were times that I couldn't even breathe for missing him and knowing that I would never see him again. Many times I would have to leave a class or a social function and run to my dorm to cry alone. I thought about him every single day and about whether I had made the right decision and tonight all these years later, I was here. It was surreal and too wonderful to let the doubts creep in. I was going to enjoy every second of tonight and if everything turned back into pumpkins at midnight, then Cinderella will have had a great evening.

We danced to several more songs and they announced that a special visitor was arriving. We made room on the dance floor and the doors opened and Santa came into the room with a giant bag. Christmas music began to play and it started to snow. It was fake snow, but snow nonetheless. It was magical. There in his arms, dancing and the snow falling on us and the lights sparkling, everything felt right in my world. If only I could keep it that way.

CHAPTER 28

We stayed until the party was over and the valet went to get his truck. It was freezing cold and he had his arm around me to keep me warm. It just felt natural at this point. I didn't want the night to end.

"Hey, you want to go have some coffee or dessert at the ice cream shop?" He asked. Maybe he didn't want it to end either.

"Sure, are they still open?"

"I think so." He said. "Let's go check it out."

We pulled into the ice cream shop, but they had closed five minutes before. He must have seen the disappointment on my face.

"I thought for sure they would be open. Gotta love small town businesses." He laughed. "Let's just go back to my house, if you want. It's still early."

"Okay, that sounds good. I'm not ready for my pretty dress to go back into the closet quite yet." I laughed.

We drove to his house and went inside. He flipped the fireplace on and turned on the Christmas tree. It might have been prettier than the party that we just left.

"Okay, hot chocolate or coffee? What'll you have?" He put cups out on the counter for us with the bag of tiny marshmallows.

"I will have hot chocolate. Coffee at this hour will keep me up all night."

"Hot chocolate it is then." He made the hot chocolate from cocoa and sugar and milk. It was heavenly. We plopped down on the couch and watched the tree lights twinkle.

He broke the silence. "Sammy, I had a really great time tonight with you. I would say it was like old times and it was, sort of, but it was better than that too. It was like perfect."

Now was the time, take the leap or run. I didn't know what to do except be honest.

"It was perfection. Everything was so pretty, just magical. I even got snow." I smiled. "But I have to be honest, I'm scared to death of tonight. "

"Why is that?" He asked.

"I'm scared of what I feel like when I'm with you again. It's like time just started over. It's always been so easy to just be myself with you. I'm scared of what might happen. I'm scared of how I feel and how you may feel. I can't bear the thought of hurting you again, and how do you feel, by the way?"

"How do I feel? You really want to know?" He asked.

"Well, I think so, but that makes me a little nervous." I tried to joke.

He moved closer to me and sat his cup on the table. "Sammy, I felt like my heart might explode when I saw you tonight. Not because you looked so beautiful, but because you have never stopped being a part of me. You moved away and we both moved on, but the moment I saw you, it was all right back in my face. I know you don't know what next week holds and I know you're torn, but I would risk my heart being crushed again, just to be with you as long as I can. If it's this week, or next or next year, it's worth it to me."

He leaned over and gently kissed me. "It makes no sense, I know, but that's how I feel. You are worth the risk to me."

I kissed him back and we leaned back on the couch with his arm around me. I was home, how could I find a way to stay? I could have sat there all night without saying another word.

CHAPTER 29

We must have fallen asleep because I woke up to the sun streaming through the living room windows. I jumped up!

"Kyle! We fell asleep! What on earth am I going to tell my dad?"

He was trying to rub his eyes open as I was yelling at him.

"Sammy, slow down. We are grown adults and we didn't do anything wrong." He laughed. "We just fell asleep. Your dad doesn't care what you do."

I stopped throwing my shoes on long enough to listen, and I started to laugh.

"You are so right! I think I bleeped back to being teenagers or something. But we should probably head toward the house. He will be wondering where we are."

"Let me change real quick and we can grab donuts and coffee on the way. Maybe bribe him a little." He said with a wink.

Was I dreaming? All those miserable days in college missing him, missing what we had and knowing that all of our dreams were forever lost. Then in two weeks, we are head over heels again. I wasn't sure where it was going or what was going to happen exactly, but I was sure that for the first time in my life, I was going to allow myself to be happy and enjoy the moment, even if the moment doesn't last.

"Are you ready to go?" He came down the stairs, skipping the last two.

"Yep, I'm ready, but I may be a little overdressed for breakfast."

"Yes, you are, but that dress deserved to be worn longer than the average dress." He held out his hand for me to take it. I took his hand and grabbed my shoes and ran out the door. It was so cold and I had no shoes or socks, but the truck warmed up fast. We got hot coffee and a box of donuts. I could only imagine how much my dad would enjoy this one.

"Hey Sal, did you think I forgot you?" Kyle said, greeting Sal as she ran off the porch to us.

"Hey Dad, I'm so sorry I didn't call you. We went back to Kyle's house and accidentally fell asleep. Sorry if I worried you." I said, embarrassed.

"You're a grown woman, Sammy. You don't owe me an explanation and you don't have a curfew. I wasn't worried."

"Alrighty then. How about a donut?" I said, surprised.

"Yea, now that sounds like a plan." He grabbed a donut and fixed his coffee. I guess he was right, I didn't owe anyone an explanation. Grow up, Sammy.

"What's on the agenda for today, Kyle?" Dad asked.

"Well, it's Saturday, so I may take the day off and spend some time with this girl I'm getting to know. So it depends on what she wants to do."

"Great idea, young man. Thinking like that will keep you happy for a long time. So what's the girl want to do?" My dad asked, looking at me.

"How do you know, he was talking about me?"

"Well, you spent the night at his house, I hope he was talking about you!" Dad teased.

Kyle came up behind me and put his arm around me, "You know I was."

This was very weird to me. I had not had a boyfriend since I left that summer, but with Kyle, it was like it was just completely normal. I still had things to prepare for the rest of my family coming, but the chance to have a day to do nothing except hang out sounded wonderful. I knew just what I wanted to do.

"I know what I want to do, or at least one thing. You can come with us dad."

"What's that?" Kyle asked.

"I want to go to the animal shelter that my mom supported. I want to see if anyone there knew her. Dad did you know she did that?"

"I do remember her saying something about it, but no details." He said.

"The lady that runs the burger place remembered me and Mom and told me how she was so sweet and how she did so much work for the animal shelter."

"Let's do it." Kyle said.

We cleaned up the kitchen and I changed out of my party dress. Sal jumped into the back of the truck and we were on our way. I was curious to see if anyone there remembered my mother. It had been years, but who knows.

The animal shelter was a small block building on a quiet road outside of town. It had a small fenced yard for the dogs to go outside, but nowhere for them to run or play. We pulled into the gravel parking lot that only had a couple of cars in it. Kyle put a leash on Sal and we went inside. It was clean but simple and plain. The girl at the desk looked up when we came in. She had on scrubs like a nurse.

"Hi, how can I help you?"

"Hello, my name is Sammy Alexander and we just wanted to stop by and visit the shelter. We have a summer house here and my mother passed away last year and one of the ladies in town told me that she helped the shelter a lot and I was just wondering if anyone here might have known her. Just sentimental I guess."

"That's so sweet," the girl said. "I have only worked here about a year, but Dr. Jane is in the back. Let me get her."

I few minutes later an older lady came out from the back and introduced herself.

"Hello, I'm Dr. Jane White. Kelly tells me your mother used to help us out here at the shelter."

"Yes ma'am, she did. Her name was Margaret "Mary" Alexander. Did you know her?

"My goodness, Mary was your mother?" She repeated. "Mary and I were very close friends. She donated a lot of her time here with these animals. She always wanted to do something great with this place, but it's on the bottom of the city budget. Let me show you something you might enjoy."

We followed her through a door and down through a hallway of dogs in cages. Some were old and some were still puppies. Most of them were two and three to a cage because there wasn't enough room. We went through another door and into Dr. White's office. She pulled a framed photo off her wall and handed it to me. It was a picture of her and my mother sitting on the ground surrounded by puppies. I couldn't help but smile. My mother looked like she was in heaven. They were laughing and the puppies were pouncing all over them.

"Look Dad, it's Mom. She was having such a good time. I'm sorry Dr. White, this is my father, John."

"Yes, Mary talked about you all the time. She hated that we never met."

My dad shook her hand and took the photo. He ran his finger along the frame.

"What kind of things did my Mary do here?" He asked.

"Oh she would do just about anything. I think I may have some other photos. Let me check." She said.

She looked in her filing cabinet and pulled out a couple of more framed photos and a small album. There were photos of my mother working at fund raisers and walking the dogs. She was really involved here. We sat in her office and looked at the photos and laughed and talked about my mother and the things she did.

Dad had been quietly looking at the photos and listening to the stories. Then He looked at Dr. White, "I would like to help the shelter too, for Mary and for the animals."

"Well, we can always use extra hands, dog food and supplies, all sorts of things." She said.

"Ok, well that's a place to start, I suppose. But I would like to do something bigger, something that would really make a difference. Maybe a fund raiser, or a pet adoption day. I will pay for whatever you need to make it happen."

"Oh my, that would be awesome, Mr. Alexander."

"Ok first, you have to call me John." He smiled.

"Hey Kyle, could we do something at the Christmas Carnival? Maybe a booth or something? What better present than a puppy or kitten for Christmas." I asked.

"Great idea, let me make a couple of calls and see what I can do."

We decided that we would figure out a way to set up a booth at the carnival for adoptions and sell some pet things like leashes, collars and treats, and each adopted pet would get free shots and spay or neuter. All of the proceeds would go to improve the shelter and we were hoping it would get others in the town more interested in getting involved. It was a great project and it was something Dad could get involved with that might keep him busy. Kyle was going to call the lady in town in charge of the booths and I was going to hit the internet to order things to sell. I could tell that Dad was excited to help with something that meant so much to Mom. I think somehow he felt like he had worked too much and had failed her in some way. We asked Dr. Jane to make a list of the ten most important things that would improve the shelter so that we would know where to start. We had a lot to do and only a week and a half to pull it together. It was going to be great.

Mom had this whole thing going on while we were all just doing our own things. She had never even mentioned it, but clearly it was important to her, or did she mention it and we just never heard her. It was nice to see photos of her being so happy, but it was sad to know that she had done all of those things alone and that we could have spent time together doing it. Somehow, I wanted to honor her, to show her she had made a difference. She never cared about being recognized by anyone, but at least she could know that we knew what she had done.

CHAPTER 30

Our next stop was Riley's for lunch, then we were going to take Dad back to the house. The little café was always crowded, but Mrs. Riley saw us and took us straight to a table. Sal wanted a burger too, but Kyle told her to wait in the truck. Mrs. Riley saw my dad and her face lit up from across the room.

"It just can't be! John Alexander, look at you!" She grabbed Dad and gave him a big squeeze. "How long has it been?"

Dad remembered her too, "Patsy Riley, how on earth are you? I can't believe you're still here working so hard. How's Bill?" The Riley's were friends of my parents when we would come to the shore in the summer. He had not seen her in years, but they started back right where they left off.

"Oh, my Bill passed a few years back and I still help my son here. I guess I don't have to work, but what am I gonna do with all that free time? Knit?" The both busted out laughing.

"I'm so sorry to hear about Bill, Patsy. He was a good man and just so much fun to be around. I'm sure you miss him."

"Yes, he was for sure, just like your sweet Mary." She said, "But you have to find a way to keep going on, don't you?"

"Yes, I suppose you do." He agreed.

We asked Mrs. Patsy to join us for lunch and she and my dad talked nonstop. We were able to tell her what we had planned for the animal shelter and she was just as excited as us. She wanted to help too, so we told her as soon as we had a plan in place she would be the first to know. She said we could put a flyer or something in her window and she would help me decorate the booth. We didn't know how successful it would turn out, but we knew it would please my mother just to know we were trying to help a place that was so special to her.

We finished lunch and Dad hugged Mrs. Patsy goodbye and she told him to please come back by and visit with her. It was so sweet to see him have such a good day. We headed back to the house just as it started to cool off.

"What a good, good day. Wasn't it a good day, Sammy?"

"Yes, Dad, it was a great day. I'm glad you had a good time and we are really going to do something great for the shelter. Mom would be very happy."

"Yes, she would I think." He agreed, "Yes she would. It really has to be great for her, Sammy."

"I know, Dad." I said looking at Kyle, "It will be, I promise."

Kyle took my hand and squeezed it tight. I knew he would find a way to make it great with me. He always had my back no matter how crazy my ideas were. He was just the kind of guy with the biggest heart that would never let a friend down.

Dad was so tired and sleepy by the time we got home. He and Sal took their normal napping positions, her by the fire and him in his chair. Kyle made some coffee and we sat on the swing with a blanket over us talking. He told me about his life when he moved to the city and how it was a good learning experience, but he knew that wasn't the life he wanted. I told him about my life of work and visiting my Dad and about Lizzy and Mac and their lives. His parents had retired and traveled a lot but they were in town for Christmas.

"Do they know I'm here yet?" I asked. I was sure that they probably hated me for leaving the way I did and for making their son so miserable.

"Yea, I told them," He said. "Of course, they were worried about me at first. I guess that's normal for parents, but they know I'm old enough to handle myself. I see them about once a week or so.

"Would you like to go visit them?"

"Gosh, I don't know if I have the guts." I laughed. "But I guess I might as well face the shooters and get it over with."

"I don't think it will be that bad. They always loved you like their own daughter, you know that."

"Yea, I know. That's one thing that makes it so hard I guess."

"Tell you what, I'm going to go home and get a shower and clean up a little and you get dressed. I will take you to a nice dinner and then we will drop by for a quick hello, nothing long or drawn out."

"Okay, that sounds nice, but let them know because no one likes people just dropping in on them unexpectedly. Especially the girl that your son was supposed to marry that has popped back up after years of being away."

"Do you have to make it sound so bad?" He laughed, "I don't even want to see you when you put it like that! My parents are the most understanding people in the world and they were the first to tell me that you had to make a hard decision."

"Alright, go change. I will be ready when you get back."

He kissed me on the forehead and headed to the truck.

"And I won't be wearing that blue sweater again," I yelled.

"I don't care what you wear. You look great regardless!"

What was I going to do with that man, and with my heart?

CHAPTER 31

I was glad I bought the sweaters and jeans. They were warm and looked great. I threw on the scarf and a pair of the earrings. The booties made me a little taller, but Kyle's 6'4" would be taller than my 5'6" no matter what I wore. I came out of my room before he got back to see Sal sleeping with Dad.

"Big plans tonight, Sammy?"

"Well, kind of," I said, hesitantly. We are going to dinner and then to see his parents. I'm pretty nervous. I hope they don't hate me for leaving like I did. Dad, I was just so young and so dumb. I just did it all wrong."

He leaned forward in his chair, "I guess everyone in the world could say that about something in their life, Sammy. The past is the past, leave it there. If other people don't want to leave it there, then that's their issue not yours. Kyle clearly wants you in his life and that's all that matters. You let your parents ruin this for you last time, don't let his ruin it this time."

"And that's part of it too, Dad. How am I going to go back home without breaking both of our hearts again? I love being with him now, but what happens after Christmas. We have a business and an office full of people depending on us, on me. It's just a lot to think about."

"Look at me, Sammy." Dad had the clearest blue eyes in the world. They could see right through you. "You enjoy yourself and don't let anyone tell you to do otherwise and the rest will take care of itself. I promise you that."

"Ok dad, I will try. You'll be okay here with Sal? I feel bad leaving you again."

"Me and Sal are just fine, aren't we girl?" Sal barely moved. "There's a movie coming on tonight I have been wanting to watch and I ate enough earlier to last me til tomorrow." He laughed, rubbing his belly.

"Knock! Knock! Ready to go?" Kyle was at the door, coming into the house.

"Yep, she's ready! Make her have fun and stop worrying. She worries too much for a young woman, you know?"

"Yes she does. I will see what I can do about that. We won't be too late."

"Bye Dad, call me if you need me."

"I won't call you or need you, now go have fun! Love you."

"Love you, too."

Kyle looked nice in his jeans and sweater and boots. It was amazing that he could work on houses all day and look like a model when he changed clothes. I don't really know how I ever got him to notice me that first summer. I was blonde haired and blue eyed with freckles on my nose. I wasn't the kind of girl that had a lot of boyfriends, but he was the kind of guy that could date any girl he wanted. He worked in town at the marina, and I was taking sailing lessons that summer so I saw him all the time, but I never had the nerve to speak. One day, he asked me about the lessons and we started talking. He had a way of putting people at ease. Then one day, he asked me if I wanted to go to the beach the next day. After that we were inseparable. I don't know why he picked me to love.

"So where are we going for dinner?" I loved all sorts of foods, but I wasn't very hungry from lunch and besides my stomach was so nervous.

"How about pizza? You do still love pizza don't you?"

He knew me too well. I could eat pizza when I wasn't hungry at all.

"I do still love a good pizza, or a bad pizza, just any pizza at all." I laughed.

We went down a side street to a small little hole-in-the-wall pizzeria that served brick oven pizza. We sat at a table in the corner beside a window. The restaurant was busy but still quiet and intimate. We ate pizza and talked about his parents. He had told them we would come by after dinner. I wasn't sure I wanted dinner to ever end. We ordered coffee and a huge cannoli to share. It was delicious.

"Okay, I can't eat another bite. Are you ready to go?" he asked.

"I'm full to the brim, but I'm not sure I'm ready to go." He took my hand and we walked to the truck and got in.

"You really are nervous about this aren't you?"

"Uh, yea, I really am. Shouldn't I be? I mean I can't imagine them being very nice and welcoming to me."

"I think you're worrying for nothing. I have never seen my parents treat anyone badly."

"Well, I guess I deserve it if they do."

"Oh my gosh! Will you stop?" He said, as he pulled over and put the truck in park. "Could you please give yourself a break, a do-over, a get-out-jail-free card or something? Look, you made a decision to help two people that you love very much. You gave up all your dreams to help those two people. Please tell me how that makes you a horrible person? You didn't have a lot of experience making big decisions and you didn't have anyone you could lean on, especially the selfish guy that was begging you to stay. You did the best you could do with the choices you had. If anyone can't see that, then they are blind."

He took my face in his hands, gently kissed me and wiped the one tear that was rolling down my cheek. He was right, I had to let the past go and see where the future took me. I had to lay down my fears and what ifs and trust that I was a good person that deserved to be happy. I was so happy right here and I was not going to spoil it.

His parents still lived in the same house, but I could tell that it had been updated. I was sure he had done it. We pulled up and he jumped out and ran around the truck to open my door.

"Okay, let's do this." I whispered taking a deep breath.

He opened the door and went inside without knocking.

"Mom, Dad? We're here. Sammy's here!"

His dad came from the den with the tv remote in his hand. He grabbed me and hugged me tight.

"Sammy! How in the world are you? You look just beautiful. Kyle, she is just as beautiful as ever!" I could feel my face turning red.

"Hi Mr. Martin, how are you? I'm doing pretty well. It's so nice to see you again."

"Kyle, is that you?" I heard from the kitchen. Mrs. Martin, came through the door. She stopped to look at me. Tears welled up in her eyes. "Sammy!" She was squeezing me close. "Sammy, it's just so good to see you again. Tell me all about yourself. How have you been? Kyle told me about your mother. I'm so very sorry to hear about her passing, she was such a kind, sweet lady. How's your father and the rest of your family. Will they be here for Christmas? We have to get together. How is your business? My goodness it's just so great to see you." She hugged me again.

"Mom, let her breathe and maybe she can answer all fifty of your questions." Kyle teased.

"I'm sorry dear," she said, "let's sit in the living room. Kyle get us some water, would you?"

"Now tell us, how have you been, Sammy? You look simply gorgeous. You have grown up."

"Yes ma'am, I suppose I have." I said.

I was very thankful for that glass of water. Kyle sat close beside me on the couch. I knew he was being protective, but after a few minutes, I wasn't nervous at all. We talked about my parents and the accounting firm, my mother's death and how my dad was moving forward. She asked about the beach house and if the entire family would be there for Christmas. We must have talked for over an hour without stopping. She seemed really happy to see me. Then she asked the question I feared the most, "When will you be leaving again dear, to go back to your job?"

"Well, I haven't exactly decided yet. I'm not sure wha…."

"You will be leaving again, right?" She looked at Kyle.

"Mom, she doesn't know when she is leaving yet. Besides, it's not your concern."

"Oh no, it's fine." I said. "I know you are concerned Mrs. Martin, but I don't have a complete plan yet. My father is thinking that he wants to live here now. Although I do have a business to run, I have realized that this town feels more like home to me than anywhere I have been in a long, long time. I don't want to hurt your son again any more than you want to see him hurt. Trust me, I worry about it every day. I didn't come back here with the plan to work things out with Kyle. I never imagined that I would even ever see him again. This is just how it worked out. I would do anything to take back any heart ache that I caused him or you and Mr. Martin, but I can't go back, I can only go forward."

She didn't answer for what seemed like hours. Then she looked at Kyle and at me and said, "I love my son with everything in me and I never want to see him hurt or disappointed, but if he loves you enough to take that chance again, I would never stand in his way. I guess you could say that none of us ever stopped loving you."

"That's so kind of you to say." I said, "You will never know how much I missed you all."

After a while, Kyle said we should be going. His parents hugged me and asked if I would come back for dinner one night and bring my dad. I told them goodnight and we headed back toward the house. I sat close to Kyle in the truck. We didn't talk, we just rode through town just being together. When he pulled into the drive, we just sat there. Finally he spoke.

"You know, Sammy, I'm not worried."

"You're not? I wish I could say that."

"I'm not worried because now I know that you feel the same as me, and that you don't want to be away from me either. I didn't know that before. I know that if we both want to be together, then we will find a way to make it happen. It will work out somehow. You do want to be with me don't you?"

"More than I have ever wanted anything. I think even more than when I left before."

"Then we will figure it out. Trust me, we will figure it out and until then, I want to soak up every possible minute with you. Could we just do that?"

"Yes, I would like that very much."

He kissed me and we got out of the car to go inside. Sal greeted us both with wet kisses and loud barks. Dad woke up when we came in the door.

"So tomorrow, let's have Christmas dinner practice." I said.

"What on earth is that?" Kyle looked at dad, curiously.

"Don't look at me." Dad laughed.

"You both know I have no idea how to cook Christmas dinner, I need to practice. It can pass as Sunday dinner for now. I will go to the store in the morning, and we can cook tomorrow afternoon for dinner. What do you want to cook, Kyle, do you have a specialty."

"Umm, steak, burgers, eggs, hotdogs, pizza...frozen."

"Ok, you're out." I laughed. "You can be my assistant!"

"Well, I'm insulted, but okay." He grinned.

"I will find some recipes and pull it together and you two can just help since you don't know how to cook any better than I do."

"Kyle, it's hard to hear, but it's the truth." Dad laughed. "I will pay for the groceries. There, that's my contribution!"

"Oh no you don't. You're not getting off that easy." Kyle pulled out his wallet.

"You two! I will pay and you will help! Plus we have to get a plan together for the shelter."

"Okay, what time do you want me here?" Kyle asked.

"Well, I don't want you to go." I teased, "But if you must, then plan to be back by lunchtime."

"I will be back and I will bring lunch with me." He smiled.

I followed him out to the porch. He hugged me close and kissed me softly.

"Goodnight, my Sammy. I will see you tomorrow."

"Goodnight."

CHAPTER 32

I woke up early, made my coffee and took my mom's journal up to her art room. I took the folded blanket off the chair, sat down and wrapped it around me. I could see why she loved it up here. She collected herself in the moments that she spent alone. My dad could be in crowds of people all the time, but not her. She loved home, she loved the quiet, and she loved just sitting and watching and taking things in. This was a perfect place for that. The view of the beach was unsurpassed. I would imagine that she could watch us playing in the ocean from those windows. I would occasionally glance toward the house and see her up there in the window painting. I would wave at her and she would wave back. We were her world. I don't ever remember her putting herself in front of anything we wanted or needed. I sat in that chair and felt happy that she had been a part of my life and that she had taught me most everything that I knew about being a good person and happy that I had this special place to visit and be close to her.

I sipped on my hot coffee and thumbed through the journal. I noticed that she had written letters to Lizzy and Mac too, but I didn't read those. She talked about missing my dad and wishing that he was there to spend more time with us. She understood his work, but she hated that he was missing the fun things that we were doing. Some of the entries made me laugh because I could see her smiling while she was writing, but others made me sad because I could feel the joy in her heart and I wished she was still there to watch her granddaughters, to take them on the beach, to make the shell necklaces.

I had an idea. I got up and got the tray of beads and shells that I had cleaned up a few days before. After snuggling back into my chair, I began to make necklaces and bracelets for my nieces. Maybe they would save them and maybe they would love the shore like she did, like I did. They knew her, but they didn't really know her. Maybe I could show them while they were here. Maybe I would be their aunt that lived near the shore. They could visit and experience summers by the ocean. I didn't know them very well, but I wanted to change that. I would change that this Christmas.

I finished what I was doing and completed my grocery list and so I just sat. I watched the waves, the birds and the few people strolling on the beach. It was like a painting. I had not painted since I left the beach years ago, but maybe I would try it again. My mother loved watercolors, but I always painted with oil. It stayed where you put it. It was predictable, forgiving. Maybe I would try the watercolors one day. I needed to let some things flow wherever they wanted to. I needed to learn that in my life.

I could hear Dad moving around down in the kitchen. I didn't want him to come back up there, so I headed down the stairs with the blanket around my shoulders. The room brought me peace, but I think it brought him regret and sadness. He couldn't yet relate to how she gained strength from that quietness but I understood completely. I had not had it in my life in a very long time, but I understood it. I had found my new solace, I would be back as soon as I had a chance.

CHAPTER 33

I searched online for recipes of foods that I thought I might possibly be able to make for Christmas dinner. Fortunately everyone in my family ate most everything so that would make it easier. I decided on ham, mashed potatoes, some kind of frozen bread, salad, green bean casserole, sweet potato soufflé and a couple of desserts. I could do this, I think. I made a list and headed to the grocery store.

I guess most people in a small town don't go grocery shopping on Sunday morning so I had the place all to myself. They were probably at church, not something that I was in the particular habit of doing. I mean, I grew up in church and I knew having a relationship with God was a good thing, but it wasn't something I focused on very much. I used to pray a lot and ask God to guide me and help me, but I gradually stopped all that when I left here and went off to college. I was starting to see how that one thing not only changed the direction of my life, but it changed me...on the inside. I guess when things get hard, people just shut off their feelings so it doesn't hurt. The problem is that you think you're only shutting off a couple of feelings about certain things or people, but gradually, everything begins to shut down. Then you wake up one day and realize, you're just here, going to work, going through the motions. This place had awoken all of my closed up places. It was scary and refreshing all at the same time. Maybe I would try talking to God again. Maybe He would still listen.

With my cart full of groceries, I headed to the register, feeling positive that I had forgotten some important ingredient. I had decided on sugar cookies and a cake for dessert.

My mother always had a day that she baked all kinds of cookies for different people and we were always required to attend the cookie decorating party, even as adults. She would bake and cut them out and we all sat around the table trying to make them look good enough to give to someone. Some of them did, ...others...not so much. I don't think she even cared about the cookies. She cared that we were all under one roof again laughing and having fun. She missed the days that we were all together.

If I could figure this out, Mac's girls could help me decorate the cookies when they got there. I wished they were coming earlier, but so far he wasn't budging about getting there before Christmas Eve. I had a lot to learn today and those men had a lot to do.

I was running late, as usual, so Kyle was already at the house when I got there. I ran an office and kept list of every detail of my life, but I was always running late. Maybe it was the little bit of my artistic mother that I actually held onto. He came out to unload the car when he heard me pull in.

"There's the chef for the day," He said. "Are you ready to do this? It's going to be great!"

"Well, you have a great attitude anyway. Are you always so positive?"

He sat the groceries down and kissed me. "As a matter of fact, I am. Thank you very much."

"So what's on the menu, Sammy? Dad asked, peeking into the bags.

"Let me get it all out and sorted, then we can start. You two wash your hands."

I took everything out of the bags and pulled out my list for dinner. Kyle started on the ham and dad started peeling carrots. We laughed and talked and cooked all afternoon. By the time it was ready, we were starving and exhausted, but dinner was superb. We all had seconds and still had enough food left over to feed an army. I had made the cake, but not the cookie cut outs. We were all too stuffed to even mention desserts. After we cleaned up the kitchen, we all crashed in front of the fireplace.

We needed to get a plan together for the shelter event, but it felt so nice just to sit on the sofa next to Kyle and watch tv. We used to watch movies all the time in the summer. There was a big place in town with an inflatable movie screen and we would take a blanket and dinner there for the movie. This little town didn't offer the night life of the city. It was slow paced and easy. I was finding that it suited me very well.

"Want to help me make cookies?" I whispered to Kyle to keep from waking up my Dad.

"Are you hungry again? It's only been an hour and a half since you ate all that food!"

"No! I'm not hungry, silly, but we need to make cookies so we can decorate them tomorrow. I want to do it with my nieces so I have to practice."

"Only you would call it practice baking just so you can have cookies."

I hit him on the arm, "You hush! And get out the cookie mix."

"Mix? You're a cookie cheater!"

"No, I am not a cookie cheater! My mom always used this mix because it was easy for cut outs and we don't have a lot of time for mess ups here."

"Alright then, let's do it."

We mixed the cookie dough up, divided it and put it in the freezer to cool it off. I remembered helping my mom and it had to be cold to make the cut outs.

We were doing just fine until Kyle threw flour at me, twice. Then it was all out war! Flour all over the kitchen, all over us and partly on Sal. I didn't remember the last time I laughed so hard. Somehow we managed to get a couple dozen cookies cut out and baked that actually looked like Christmas trees and gingerbread men and weren't burned to a crisp or eaten by Kyle. It took forever to clean up the kitchen, and it was late when we finished, so Kyle decided to head on home.

"You know, we actually have to get some work done tomorrow."

"I know, I know." I said as I leaned up against him. He hugged me close.

"I will call the lady over the Christmas Carnival in the morning before I come over if you want."

"Yea that would be great. Thanks. I guess I will see you in the morning then."

"I guess you will", He hugged me tight. "Goodnight"

"Night, see you in the morning."

CHAPTER 34

We spent the next afternoon with him working on the house and me standing behind him asking questions and planning the booth for the carnival. We got the okay from the city, in fact, they loved the idea. We had to get busy. The booths would already be set up, but we had to come up with things to sell and some good ideas to get some puppies and kittens adopted. I decided to shop around on the internet and dad put up the money for the stock of leashes, collars and other items. I bought everything from bones to bows. We also needed extra crates to keep the dogs and cats in at the carnival. It would be here before we knew it and I still had things to do on the house.

My plan was to clean out Mom's craft room for the girls to sleep in, but I just loved it so much like it was. I needed a new plan, at least until after Christmas, then I would have to make a decision about her things. I wanted to leave it like it was until Lizzy and Mac got there. I needed a place to put two little girls a bed. Maybe Kyle could help me think of something. I told him what I was thinking and he looked around like he had lost something.

"Well, I'm good, but I can't build you a room in a week." He said. "Let's take a look and see what we can figure out."

We walked around the house looking in every room. The house had three bedrooms, the living room, and the kitchen with a small dining room off to one side.

"What's in here?" He asked.

"It used to be a small laundry area and it held the washer and dryer, but then dad had an actual laundry room built because Mom hated it."

"I have an idea," Kyle said.

"You do? Of course you do? What's your idea?"

"I can build them two small bunks in here in a day. Kids love bunk beds!" He was so excited.

"Oh my goodness, that's perfect!" I hugged him. "You're the greatest!"

"And don't you forget it! I will pick up some wood in the morning and you can get a couple of mattresses pretty cheap."

"That's so great. It will be so good for them."

"When you finish today, let's go see if we can find some sheets and stuff so as soon as you get them made, I can pull it all together."

"Sounds like a plan. You're dad want to come and grab some dinner?" He asked.

I told Dad about our plan, and he loved it. He agreed to go eat if we went back to Riley's Burgers. He said he really enjoyed talking with Mrs. Riley about old times and had told her he would come back by there soon. Kyle finished up his work and took some measurements for the beds and we set out. There was a small department store right outside of town that had the mattresses, sheets, pillows and blankets. I found navy quilts and white sheets with navy sea shells on them and a throw pillow for each bed. Kyle said we could hang a curtain for them to pull shut at night, so I found a thick navy curtain that would block the light from the other room. We got two night lights to mount on the beds. I loved doing this. I had planned to spend my life decorating houses. It wasn't work to me. I liked to see an empty room come alive with personality and welcome its guests. I realized that I had not even enjoyed decorating my own condo this much. It was a really nice place, but it wasn't a place that I ever spent time at and it didn't feel like a home. It just felt like a place where I kept my stuff. . Funny how when one part of life shuts down, the whole thing follows.

We took dad back to visit with Mrs. Riley and Kyle and I walked over to the coffee shop while they were still talking. It was too cold to sit outside so we grabbed a table by the front window so we could see the boats at the marina. The sun was going down just as we sat down. The boats were swaying back and forth with the evening wind and you could hear the sailboat masts dinging with the slap of the ropes. I could sit there for hours.

"So how do you ever get anything done living at this place? I asked. "I'm afraid I would want to skip work and go to the beach every single day."

"I promise you, some days are worse than others. My worst time is the spring, after a cold winter and we have a hot, sunny day or in the fall after the tourists have all gone home and the weather starts to turn just a little cooler. Then I want to load that old surf board in the truck and see if I can still catch a wave." He smiled looking out at the water.

"And can you?" I asked. "I'm sure that I can't even stand up on a board anymore."

"Just like riding a bike." He assured me. "You were good at it. I'm sure you could still handle it."

"Soooo, I have a question for you Mr. Martin."

"Okay, Mr. Martin is my dad, but go ahead."

"So how many hearts have you stolen in this small town over the years? Any girls watching me around the corner?"

"To my knowledge, I have not taken any hearts." He laughed. "I dated everybody here in high school! And besides, by the time I moved back, they were all married. To be honest, I never dated much in the city either. Spent most of my weekends with a hairy girl named Sally the Golden Retriever."

"Well, count your blessings because I spent most of mine with an adding machine."

"Never dated?" He asked.

"Just an occasional, office party that I needed to bring someone to, but nothing serious. Matter of fact, guess what?"

"What?" He was curious.

"I have never even kissed anyone besides you in all these years." I waited for his reaction.

"No way? He seemed surprised.

"Nope"

"I guess that's a good thing. No competition for me that way." He teased.

"Do you think it's crazy we ended up back here, together."

"I like to think it's fate working for us and not against us. And maybe your momma up in heaven pushing things around a bit. She did always like me better if you remember."

"I do remember. She thought you were great. I found an old journal that she had in her room upstairs. She had written me a letter in it. I don't know if she ever planned to give it to me or if she was just saying all the things that she couldn't say in person, but it was pretty cool to find it. She wrote Lizzy and Mac one too, but I didn't read there's."

"Wow! That is so awesome. I remember walking with you on the beach and you could look up to that room and see her in the window working or painting. I know you miss her so much."

"Funny, when I'm at the shore, I don't miss her nearly as much as when I'm home."

"Sammy, what are we going to do after Christmas? We have to think of something. There has to be a way to make this work. Clearly, we both just go through the motions of life without each other. Are we just supposed to relive the same scene from years ago all over again?"

"I don't know what the answer is, Kyle. I have a business now and other people depending on me with families. They need their jobs. It's not just about me."

"I get that." He said, "Really I do, but just answer me two questions."

"One: When does your life get to be about you? And Two: Do you want to find a way to make this happen?"

"Okay, One: I'm not sure how to make my life about me, but I'm trying a little bit, and two: I want to find a way to make this happen more than I have ever wanted anything."

He smiled and took my hand, looked me straight in the eye and said, "Okay, as long as we are on the same page about being together, I can figure out a way. I don't know how yet, but I know you didn't just fall back into my life for no reason."

"I hope you're right," I said.

CHAPTER 35

Kyle came over early to finish one job and then start on the beds. I was so excited. It was going to be awesome. Dad and I were going back to the shelter to update and meet with Dr. Jane and pull the details of the carnival together. I had not seen him excited about anything like this in a long time, if ever. He was concerned that people wouldn't respond and they wouldn't make enough money to really help the shelter.

As we rode over, he said, "Hey Sammy, I would like to do something extra for the shelter. You know, to make sure they have what they need."

"What do you want to do dad?"

"Well, when your mother passed, I had an insurance policy and I invested some of it, but I just put the rest in an account. I don't need it Sammy, and I think it would be great to support something that your mom loved so much. I think that would have been what she would want to do with it. What do you think?"

"Dad, I think that would be the most awesome thing ever and I think mom would have loved it. How do you want to do it?"

"I don't know yet, but I don't want some big fanfare. I don't want it to be made public."

"Dad, how much money are we talking about here? I thought you meant a couple thousand dollars or something."

"No, more like a fifty thousand dollar donation. I know it's a lot, but it's my money and that's what I want to do with it."

"Okay, Dad, you don't have to defend it. If that's what you want to do then that's what we will do. Dr. Jane is going to flip!"

We spent a few hours with Dr. Jane at the shelter, just getting a feel for things and how they operate. There were a few paid employees and a couple of volunteers. It was a no kill shelter, so there were quite a few animals that needed adoption. The place was clean and the animals were well cared for, but they depended on volunteers to take them on walks and play with them, so they spent a lot of time in their cages. It made me so sad to see all of them without homes. Hopefully what we were doing would make a big difference. She told us that they owned the grass lot next door but the dogs had to stay on leashes to keep them from running away.

I told her about all the things I had ordered and that I hoped the rest of my family would help us the days of the carnival. She was going to see if any of the employees and volunteers might take a short shift too. I told her I would let her see the stuff when it came in and we would figure out a way to set it all up.

"John, Sammy, I just can't think you enough. You're just an answer to my prayers! This is just going to be so fantastic."

"We are so excited, Dr. Jane. It will be here before you know it. We are happy to help. I know my mom has a big smile on her face right now."

She hugged us goodbye and we told her we would be in touch later in the week. I needed to get home and start on those cookies and see how the bunk beds were coming.

CHAPTER 36

Kyle had finished the beds in only a few hours! They looked so good and fit perfectly into the little hallway laundry area. He was cleaning up when we came inside.

"Well, what do you think?"

"I think you are fantastic!" I said, giving him a hug and a kiss.

He smiled, "well, a guy will work all day for that!"

"They are so perfect, can we put the mattresses on yet?" I was actually super excited to put my sheets and pillows on.

"Let me fix the lights we bought first then you can go at it."

"Okay, I'm going to make a sandwich, want one?"

"I will meet you on the porch in fifteen minutes." He said.

"It's a date." I smiled.

Dad decided to go to the beach for a quick walk while I made lunch. In the back of my head I remembered that I needed to call Howard back at the office just to double check on things. I had already overnighted the signed checks for everyone's Christmas bonus and he knew how to add their hours for the paid time off, but I still needed to touch base with him. We texted and emailed back and forth over the week, but I liked to talk in person too.

Kyle and I sat down on the porch and I wanted to tell him about my dad's donation for the shelter before he came up from the beach. My dad would get embarrassed if Kyle said anything about it, but I wanted to share it with him. He couldn't believe my dad wanted to do that.

"Didn't he used to be kind of tight with his money?"

I laughed, "Yea, I guess he did. I don't even know who he is anymore, or maybe I'm starting to know the real person my mom fell in love with before careers and jobs and business took over."

"Yea, maybe so. I don't want to do that."

"Do what?" I didn't know what he meant.

"Let those things take over my life and change me. I know it's important, but where does it end? How do you stop the roller coaster? How do you hit the reset button?"

"I'm not sure," I said, "I will let you know when I figure it out."

Dad walked up onto the porch with Sal and dusted the sand off his shoes.

"Got some sandwiches, Sammy?"

"Right here dad, waitin' for ya."

"Glad we are here together," he said, "I want to talk to you both about something."

"Is something wrong?"

"No, no." He looked at Kyle, "she always thinks something is wrong."

"Okay, no I don't"

"Yea you do," Kyle agreed.

"Alright, you two, stop ganging up on me. What's up dad?"

"Well, I mentioned it before, when we first got here, but you brushed me off. I was serious when I said I wanted to live here, Sammy.

"But dad.."

"Now let me finish. I don't know exactly how it can work and I know you do a lot of things to help me around the house, but I feel stronger here, more alive. My arthritis doesn't hurt so much and I don't feel the stress of the business. I just want you to think about it. You are happier than you have ever been and I will not let you toss that aside again. There is nothing there for us, Sammy. Yea we have an office and some employees, but nothing for our life. I don't quite know the answer, but I do know for sure that I want to find one."

Then he turned to Kyle, "And since you have been working on the house, I need for you to do a complete inspection and see what kind of work it really needs. I would like to make some updates. Nothing major, just some painting and maybe some kitchen and bathroom stuff."

"I would be happy to help you with whatever I can, John, and honestly the updates would help even if you decided to sell the house."

"Hello! Does anyone remember that the business you all are talking about is my source of income? And Dad, you get a hefty retirement check each month from there too. How am I supposed to make a living with an accounting degree in this little town?"

Kyle laughed, "We pay taxes too you know. But I have a better idea."

"Oh, I'm sure you do."

"Let's hear it, Kyle!" Dad said.

"Why don't you do what you have always wanted to do? Why don't you design and decorate the homes and businesses that I update?"

"Kyle, that's just a dream job. I don't even have any experience."

"You gotta start somewhere. Lots of people start things on a dream. I believe in you. I know you can do it!"

"So you're determined to live in this house?" I looked at my dad.

"I am, Sammy. There's not a reason in the world that I can't. I know you worry about me, but you worry too much. I have some old friends here and I can make some new ones. I'm not asking for your permission."

"Oh I am well aware of that fact, but I don't know where to start to make that a reality. Do either of you?"

"I think you have to decide if you still want to be involved in the company or not. If not, I will sell it to one of the top accountants there and move on. If so, you can do what you want with it. I guess you could put someone under you to be there full time and you could manage that person from here like you have been doing."

"Well, this has worked for a few weeks, in a down time, but you and I are the faces of that company. I don't know how long it would last with me working from another state."

"I honestly don't care, Sammy. The only thing that matters to me is that you are taken care of and doing what you want to do. If it's work the business I will support you and if it's walk away and do your own thing, then I will support that too."

"Okay, dad, let me think about it a couple of days."

"Think all you want." He said. "Kyle, you do that inspection whenever you're ready and tell me the damage. Sal and I are going to take our nap." He got up and went into the house and leaned back in his chair.

Kyle and I just sat there stunned. I couldn't believe my dad had just made up his mind like that. I knew that I was one decision away from leaving everything at home and following my heart for the first time ever. It felt a little scary and strangely peaceful. But did I really have the nerve to jump?

CHAPTER 37

After I got the bunk beds made, pillows in place and the curtain hung, I felt like I could decorate the White House. It looked so nice and the girls were simply going to love it. I was going to pick up a few books and put them in a basket under the bottom bunk for them to read at night with their nightlights that Kyle had mounted to the headboards.

"Guess what?" I turned to Kyle.

"As soon as you get all your tools picked up, we can decorate those cookies we made last night."

"That sounds messy and delicious." He said.

"Guaranteed to be both."

"Let me get my stuff up and I will be right there."

"Okay, I will pull all the stuff out."

I bought icing and icing bags, food coloring, and every sparkling thing I could find at the grocery store. I set it all out on the counter and covered the counter with paper and placed the cookies on the paper. I was ready to go.

"Okay, let's do this." He came over and grabbed a plain cookie and shoved it in his mouth.

"Okay buddy, don't eat the cookies."

"Sammy, did you just hear yourself? What kind of rule is that? Cookies are made to be eaten. That's their one job." He teased.

"Yea, maybe you're right." As I crammed a cookie into my mouth.

"That's my girl." He said.

"Am I?"

"Are you what?"

"Am I your girl?"

"Sammy, I'm pretty sure you have always been my girl." He said leaning toward me.

"I'm glad." I smiled as he kissed me.

We knew nothing about decorating cookies. Absolutely nothing. Having said that, the cookies didn't turn out half bad. They weren't cookie shop material, but they were fun and tasty. The girls would absolutely love doing this. At least I hope they loved it. I didn't know them very well because they didn't live close, but we skyped and I sent them gifts on birthdays. Mac let them have a relationship with my dad even though their relationship wasn't very good at all. Maybe time had healed some things and Dad was a little more thoughtful before speaking his mind these days. I hoped that they would patch things up during this trip.

Kyle was getting ready to head home when he remembered that he had bought me something. He had left it in his truck. He came back in with a small package in a brown paper back. It looked like a book.

"I thought you might enjoy one of these of your own." He said, handing me the package.

"What is it? You know I love presents!"

I pulled the book out of the bag and it was a brown leather journal with a leather strap that wrapped around it. I used to journal when I first started college, but that, like everything else, stopped the year after I left him.

"Kyle, I love it!" I hugged it close. "This was just the most thoughtful gift ever."

"I knew you used to like to write in your journal and when you said your mom had written you a letter, I thought you might enjoy it again."

"I will, I love it so much. Thank you." I hugged him.

"You are very welcome. Maybe it will help you sort out your thoughts. I will see you tomorrow." He kissed me again and headed out the door.

"Let's go, Sal. You don't live here, you know."

Sal jumped to her feet to follow him out the door. She stopped to let me hug her goodnight and ran out after him.

CHAPTER 38

I was more like my mother than I have ever even realized. I did love writing in my journal. Nothing secretive or important, just my thoughts about whatever might have been happening in my life at the time. Dad was asleep so I slipped up the steps, and headed to her chair with my journal.

I guess I wrote like my mom too, in letter form, but most of my stuff was more like letters to God or prayers. I sat down in her chair and watched some tiny lights out on the ocean. It was cold and windy, but I assumed it was fishing boats of some kind. It was black everywhere except for those two tiny white lights and one red one. I wondered if those people on the boats lived here and if their families worried about them being out there in the dark cold water.

I turned on her lamp beside the chair and threw the blanket over my legs. The room was almost eerie at night with the house so quiet. I opened the journal and wrote the date at the top of the first page. I began to write about how I felt being here at the shore, being at this house and being with Kyle again. I wrote about feeling close to my mother and how my father had changed. How he wanted to move to this house and how I would love to be here with Kyle. The words poured out of me like I was talking to a long lost friend. I wrote about Lizzy and how I wished I could see her more often. I talked about Mac and how I hoped that he and Dad could repair their relationship and the girls could visit us more. As I wrote, I laughed and cried. All these new feelings were strange to me. My feelings normally consisted of being nice to people at work, and the grocery store and going home alone. Not much to feel about that.

I decided to turn in early. It had been a busy few weeks and I had been running strong every single day. I rested so well here at night, but I was tired. I looked forward to going to bed before midnight. I took my new journal and wrapped the string around it, cut off the lamp and headed downstairs to bed.

Dad was still asleep in his chair, so I woke him up to tell him to go to bed, and put out the fire.

I climbed into bed and took out my mother's journal and flipped to the middle where I had been reading. She was writing about helping at the shelter and how she and Dr. Jane had become such good friends. Dr. Jane loved the animals and spent even her own money to take care of them because there was so little funding from the city. Mom was trying to come up with a fund raiser idea. She wished that she could take all the dogs and cats home with her so they would feel safe and like they belonged to someone. She had a way of making everyone feel liked they belonged to her and that she would take care of them. She wrote about how it would be when she and dad finally got to move to the beach house too. She looked forward to having their coffee on the porch together and walking on the beach each evening. She hoped to spend more time painting and hoped that he would find some hobby besides work that he would enjoy. She planned to have her grandchildren come for the entire summer the way we used to, so that they could learn to love the ocean too. They would pick up shells and make necklaces and bracelets, build sand castles and then walk to town for ice cream. She had so many dreams and plans that she never got to see. Maybe I could do some of those things for her. I must have been exhausted because I fell asleep with her journal on my chest. That night I dreamed that Kyle and I got married on the beach in front of the ocean.

CHAPTER 39

I must have slept really late because I woke up to someone banging on the front door. What on earth, Kyle always came in the screened porch door? I jumped out of bed and peeked out the window through the blinds. It was the mail delivery guy and I had to sign for packages. I still had on my pajamas with crazy hair.

"Wait! I'm coming! Don't leave please!" I yelled.

I ran down the hall and through the house and flung the door open. I must have looked crazy from the look on his face.

"Good morning ma'am, got some packages for you. Need your signature though."

"Ok, yea." I could barely see him for the bright sun shining behind him into my eyes. "Where do I sign?"

"Right there on the line, ma'am. Where should I put all these packages?"

I had him put them all in stacks in the dining room because it was empty except for the table and chairs. There were so many boxes and I was still half asleep.

"What in the world?" Dad came into the room.

"Did you sleep late too?" I asked. "It's all the stuff I ordered for the shelter to sell at the Christmas Carnival."

He finally finished bringing in all the boxes and Dad was making coffee, so I wondered back to my room to get dressed. It was 9 o'clock. I hadn't slept that late in six or seven years. It felt great! I got dressed and presentable and went to get that cup of coffee.

I stood there eyeing all those boxes not having the slightest idea of what I was going to do with all that stuff. I decided that my walk on the beach was first, then I would deal with that. There were a few more people out on the beach than normal. I guess because I was usually out there by seven thirty. It was still pretty empty though. It seemed like it got colder every day. I had to wear a hat and gloves just to walk down the beach now. It was still beautiful to me though. I walked a good way and found an old tree that somehow had landed far enough up on the sand to get stuck and dry out. I sat down on it and just listened to the waves and the birds. I watched the seagulls swoop and land, looking for a leftover cracker on the sand or a small fish in the water. A group of pelicans glided right over the crest of the waves looking for their breakfast. They were so big and always flew in their V pattern. The sun sparkled on the blue water like jewels. I was lost in the view when a big fluffy dog came bounding up to me.

"Well, hello there, buddy. Where did you come from?"

I looked up to see if he had an owner and a man was walking toward me.

"Hello, how are you?" He said. "Sorry about that, he saw you and took off running. Normally he stays right with me."

The dog looked like a big sheepdog with a red sweater on. He was adorable.

"That's okay," I said as I shielded my eyes from the sun so I could see who I was talking to. It was an older man in a red jogging suit.

"How are you?" He said. "Having a good morning?"

"Yes, I am, how about you?" I answered as I kept petting the dog.

He explained that he tries to come out early before many people get to the beach so his dog can run and play and chase his ball.

"Has anyone ever told you that you look like..?

"Like Santa Clause?" He finished my sentence. "Yes, they do. It's the white beard I suppose. I used to dress up years ago, but since my wife and I moved here I stopped doing it. We just love Christmas, but no reason to dress up like Santa for your puppies I guess." He laughed.

"No, I guess not," I agreed and smiled. "Did you say puppies? You have more than one dog."

"Oh yea, we love dogs, we have five, but I can't let them all go at once and he minds me better than the rest."

"So you love dogs, huh?"

"Oh yea, all of our dogs are rescue dogs. Just can't stand the thoughts of them not having a home."

"Are you serious? I know you don't know me, but we are doing a fund raiser for the local shelter and I think I have a great idea that we could really use your help with, if you're interested."

"I will sure help if I can. What is it?"

I told him all about the shelter and the carnival and how we were going to raise money and about all the stuff I bought, but I couldn't figure out a good way to really get people interested even though this was a very dog friendly town.

"So I was just thinking, what if we did pictures with Santa for your pet? Maybe while people are standing in line, they would shop for the other items."

"Oh honey, we would love to do something like that for the animals."

"We?"

"Yes, me and my wife. She dresses up like Mrs. Clause!"

"You've got to be kidding me! How did I get so lucky today?"

He gave me his number and said to call him with the details of the time and place and that he would get his wife to pull out their costumes and get them ready. I could not believe this was happening. I practically ran back to the house to tell my dad. He and Kyle were on the porch drinking coffee when I ran up.

"Did you run on the beach this morning? Kyle asked, confused because I never ran anywhere.

"I ran back here to tell you both something."

They thought it was a great idea and couldn't believe how it all fallen into place.

"I know, it's crazy. One minute I'm sitting there looking at the ocean and the next minute I'm meeting Santa...and his dog!" We all laughed. "But I think it will be an excellent way to draw people to our booth. We need to advertise that the most on our flyers too, so that people can look forward to doing it."

I ran inside to get my computer to start working on the flyer. We only had a week to get the word out and get people excited.

"Get your walking shoes on boys. We are going to have flyers to hand out by lunchtime."

They both decided they would need a second cup of coffee while I typed away without looking up. I had to make sure those dogs and cats were taken care of and I had figured out a way to do it.

"Thanks for your help, Mom." I said to myself. I wasn't sure about my relationship with God at the moment, but if guardian angels were a thing, then I knew she was watching over me.

CHAPTER 40

We started early the next day covering the town with flyers. Because Kyle knew everyone in the town, we were able to post them in almost every store and restaurant in the entire town. We took them to neighborhoods and put them on mailboxes and we took some by the shelter for Dr. Jane and the staff to hand out. She loved the idea.

We finally got back to the house after lunch and Kyle started his inspection of the house while I started opening all the boxes. I was about half way through when the phone rang.

"Hello!"

"Hey Sis! How's it going?" It was Mac. He never called. We loved each other, but we mostly communicated through Amy. "How's the beach?"

"Heeey! I'm good and the beach is great! How are you? Is something wrong?" I asked, realizing that my Dad and Kyle were right about me worrying too much.

"No, we are all okay, it's just about the beach trip. I'm just not sure about coming and being stuck in a house for three or four days with Dad and us barely even speaking to each other."

"Yea, I understand, really I do." I tried to sound compassionate, "But Dad is different, Mac. I promise it won't be like that. He has been so different since we got here. He doesn't even care about the business now."

"Our dad doesn't care about that business?" he asked, "I think someone must have switched him out when you weren't looking."

I told him about closing the office for Christmas and paying the employees and giving them their bonus too and about wanting to move to the beach and even selling the business if he had to. Mac couldn't believe his ears. He was very driven too, but in an effort to keep from being like dad, Mac learned to balance family and work. He was still a workaholic but he tried to spend more time with his girls doing special things. I also told him about the Christmas Carnival, the shelter and the things I had planned for the girls.

"Man, you have been a busy girl, haven't you?"

"Yea I have and we have been having work done on this house too."

"Really, how did you find someone on such short notice? It takes forever around here for a handy man to get time for a new customer."

"Kyle is doing it," I said quietly.

"Who? Kyle who?" he asked. "Oh my gosh, Sammy, Kyle Martin?"

"The one and only." I said. Mac liked Kyle a lot and he hated to see me leave him.

"Man, I never thought I would hear that name again." He said.

I filled him in on how Kyle had moved away then moved back and how he bought the bungalow, but never did anything to it until finally he needed a place to live. We talked about how neither one of us had ever really dated anyone else and how we had picked up right where we left off.

"Well, little sister, it looks like I'm going to have to make a trip to the beach just to keep up with the goings on of my family!" He joked.

"Yes! You definitely do. I would love it if you could come for just one extra day. Maybe the day before Christmas Eve. Maybe Christmas Eve Eve?" We always called it that growing up.

"I won't promise anything. It's crazy around here, but I will talk to Amy"

"Okay good enough," I said. "I can't wait to see you guys."

"Me too, Sis. I will see you next week."

"Okay, love you."

"Love you too."

"Hey, Sammy?"

"Yea?"

"Tell Dad I'm looking forward to catching up."

"I will, Mac, he will be so happy!"

Dad just stood there with tears in his eyes when I told him.

"This is going to be the best Christmas, Sammy. I never thought I would get a second chance to get things right with Mac, but I am getting that chance, aren't I?"

"Yes, I think you are Dad," I said as I hugged him.

Mom always said, "don't miss out on a chance to right a wrong, Sammy."

Today, I knew just what she meant.

CHAPTER 41

I was so happy to hear from Mac. I missed him. Lizzy was the baby and we probably treated her like that even though she was only a few years younger than either of us. Mac and I had already established a strong bond before she came along. I was a little bit of a tomboy, so we did everything together as kids. Lizzy liked girly things and hated getting dirty or getting her clothes messed up, so she never hung out with us. If Mac did it, I was right on his heels.

I unpacked the boxes and made signs for each item. I separated them by style and color and put them in individual baskets that I found at the market. I had almost everything ready for the booth except we needed some sort of big chair for Santa to sit in while people took pictures of their dogs with him on their cell phones. I had no idea where to find something like that. Maybe someone had something they would let us use for a couple of days. Maybe Kyle knew someone.

We would also need good treats to get the dogs to sit still with Santa. I was going to have my hands full for a few days.

Kyle finished the inspection after about an hour and came down out of the attic.

"Well, what's the damage son?" Dad asked.

"Actually there is one big thing and a few small things, but that is all I found. This house is solid as a rock. You need a new roof and I have a guy that can inspect it and possibly get your home insurance to cover part of it because it's mostly caused by storms over the years. You need to update your hot water heater and blow a different kind of insulation into the attic that is up to the new standard, but that's about all I saw other than cosmetic things like painting the outside, maybe adding some stronger storm shutters, and cutting back some tree limbs that have grown over the top of the house."

"When can you start on that and the remodel?" Dad asked.

"Dad, are you in a hurry or something?" I said.

"Well, if I'm going to live here, then I want it fixed as soon as possible."

"Can we wait until after Christmas at least?" I said.

Kyle looked at me and winked, "Yea, it would be better to wait until after the holidays to schedule people to come out and look at things. The whole town is involved in that carnival and things kind of shut down here the week before Christmas and it's already Thursday."

"Okay, if you say so," Dad said, "you're the boss."

"Well, I don't get called that very often," Kyle said.

"Thank you," I whispered. "When he gets something on his mind, he just won't stop until it's taken care of and he isn't used to breaking for Christmas.

It seemed that dad had seriously made up his mind about moving. I wasn't sure what that looked like for either of us, but he was a grown man and he knew what he wanted. I knew enough to not waste my time arguing with him either. I would not win. He would have to change his doctors, and his house, of so many years, would have to be packed up or sold and his things moved to somewhere....who knows where. He acted like he could just stay here and buy some new clothes and forget the rest of his life back home. But it just wasn't that simple for either of us, or was it? Maybe I made things too hard with my overthinking. Truth be known, if I thought about something too long, I always talked myself out of it. Just jump for once in your life, Sammy.

CHAPTER 42

We spent the entire weekend getting the house finished and ready for everyone to arrive. We went grocery shopping, together, which was quite an adventure. Kyle was like a five year old wanting every cookie in the store, but it was fun. It was different getting to know him and his personality as an adult. We weren't adults before, we were both so young we had not fully developed our personalities. Most young couples also don't grocery shop together, so this was a real treat. I found out that he loves chips and ice cream, not together, but loves them. We bought half the store and loaded it all into his truck. I needed enough food for several meals and snacks for everyone.

I also had a couple of other Christmas presents to pick up for Dad and Kyle, but I didn't want him to see his. I had to make a trip back to town to get it one morning before he came over. By Sunday evening, we were exhausted.

Kyle invited Dad and me over to his house for dinner and I was excited for Dad to get to see his house. Also, he was cooking, so that was a win-win for me. We arrived before the sunset so

Dad could view it in all its glory. He remembered the nice street as I made the turn to go down to Kyle's.

"Always the prettiest street in this little town." He said. "It's funny that Kyle bought you a house on this street so many years ago." He winked at me.

"Dad! He didn't buy it *for* me, but I do love it so much."

The road seemed to run right on top of the sand and the dunes were low so the view of the ocean was limitless. It wasn't a well-known, popular beach, so only the locals came during the summer. There also wasn't a lot of parking available so that limited the people too. It seemed like the entire beach only belonged to the few houses on that street. It wasn't my home, but it sure felt like it could be.

Kyle greeted us at the door with a couple of blankets and some hot chocolate. "What's all this for?" Dad asked.

"It's for watching the show," Kyle said. "Should be a good one."

We sat down on the chairs and swing on his front porch and sipped our hot chocolate. The blankets were great because it had already started cooling off.

We were all talking when Kyle spoke, "Look at that John."

My dad looked up and caught his breath, "Wow, I don't know if I have ever seen a more beautiful sunset. All the colors are just breathtaking. You get to see this every night?"

"Well, every night that I'm not at your house." He laughed.

We watched until the last sliver of light was gone behind the dark water, then we headed inside. Kyle had a fire going and all of his Christmas lights turned on. Whatever he was cooking smelled delicious.

"Kyle, your tree and lights look fantastic."

"You can thank your daughter for all that. She forced me to buy a tree and decorate. Turns out my neighbors seem to like me more too."

"She definitely has a knack for pulling things together in a house." Dad said.

"That reminds me, Sammy, would you have time to ride over to an office with me tomorrow and give me some decorating ideas. I am remodeling the space but it has to be set up for various businesses to be able to rent the offices within the building. The owner wants me to just handle it all."

"Yes, she has time." Dad interrupted.

"Dad, mind your manners."

"Well, you want experience. There you are!" Dad said.

"Yea, I guess I could go with you to look at it. Maybe I could come up with something."

"Good! Now, who's hungry?" Kyle said as he took the lid off a huge pot.

He had made pot roast with vegetables, corn bread, and a salad on the side. It looked as good as it smelled.

"Did you cook all this?" Dad was impressed.

"You learn to cook when you live alone in a town with three restaurants and a lot of seafood places." Kyle joked.

"Sammy, you better keep him, he cooks better than you do!"

"He sure does," I winked at Kyle, "I think he was faking when we cooked our practice Christmas dinner. Acting like he didn't know how to do anything."

"It was your show. I was just an assistant." He laughed.

Dad wanted to know what Kyle had done to the house since he bought it so Kyle pulled out some "before" photos to show us. It was amazing. No one had lived in the house for years and because of the location being off the main beach, and no one had rented it for vacation either. It was a well-kept secret. The owners were older and had passed away and he bought it for a bargain from the bank, but it was in shambles. The city would have probably torn it down, but restoration was right up Kyle's alley. He replaced the front porch, the floors, the living room and a lot of the insides. Everything that didn't need replacing got an update except the old shiplap on two of the living room walls. Turns out, the restoration of this house got him enough attention to be hired by the city for the other restoration projects. His work was remarkable.

We finished dinner and he had made brownies with vanilla ice cream for dessert. We were stuffed and relaxing on the sofa when he pulled out an old photo album full of photos of us. I had not seen any of these pictures of us since the summer I left, besides the few he had in the box. I don't know if mom packed them up with other things from my old room or if she threw them away. We looked so young and so happy. Sailing, playing on the beach, surfing and just being together. Seeing those brought back every feeling I was having when they were taken. Where did that girl go? How did this worrying, planning, OCD woman develop from that sun kissed, fun loving, free spirited girl in those photos?

Soon it was time to go. I kissed Kyle goodnight and Dad and I headed home, or back to the beach house. Was it home?

CHAPTER 43

Looking at the building with Kyle was so inspiring. It was an office space with a main lobby that needed decorating to accommodate any client. I took measurements on the space and wrote down some notes. It was a space right on the main street of town, so the large windows looked out over the city green space and marina. I literally had no idea what I was doing, but I loved trying it and I didn't have anything to lose because if Kyle didn't like what I did, no one else would ever see it, right? We walked around the building with him showing me the layout and where all the rooms would be. The offices would decorated by the client that rented them, but the main lobby needs a modern style that still fit with the beach town. I was like a wide-eyed little girl looking around and letting ideas pop into my head.

"This is so exciting for you, isn't it?" Kyle said.

"It's crazy, but it just feels so great, my heart is racing!" He hugged me tight.

"I know you can do this, Sammy. You were born to do this."

"I so hope you're right." I said, as we walked to his truck.

We stopped back by the shelter to touch base with Dr. Jane and see if she was ready for the big fundraiser. She greeted us at the door with a hug. She was so excited about all the items to sell and especially about Santa coming for photos. There were several staff people and volunteers there bathing the dogs and getting them ready for a hopeful adoption. We had bows for all the dogs and cats so that they would look extra cute.

When we left, it was almost time for dinner, so we grabbed Chinese on the way back and sat in front of the fire with dad and Sal to eat.

"I'm really looking forward to seeing Lizzy tomorrow." Dad said.

"Meee too!" I agreed. "I haven't seen her in forever. We video chat every couple of weeks, but that's not the same."

"Does she know I'm still lurking around?" Kyle asked.

"Lurking?" I laughed, "Is that what you're doing? That sounds so creepy."

He grabbed my leg, "You know what I mean, silly. Does she know I still live here and that we have been doing things together again."

"As a matter of fact she does."

"And?"

"And she told me to follow my heart and stop listening to my head and all of the facts that should look like the right answer." I said, with a smirk.

"Always liked that girl," Kyle teased.

"Well, she will be here TOMORROW afternoon, so you can tell her yourself."

"Is she married?" Kyle asked.

"Yea, she is, but her husband works all the time and she said he isn't coming with her, not even for Christmas."

"Married her daddy, I guess." Dad said.

"You were just working hard to give us all a good life, Dad. Don't be so hard on yourself."

"The problem with that, Sammy, is that it starts that way for sure, but then you get used to a certain lifestyle and you have to spend the rest of your life working to keep up with it. Then it just becomes a habit and you don't know what to do with yourself unless you're working sixty hours a week."

"Well, maybe he will find a balance, and they can work it out."

"That's the pot calling the kettle black isn't it?" Dad teased.

"Hush!" I said.

Dad was excited to see Mac and Amy and the girls too. He hadn't said much, but he had asked several times if we had enough Christmas gifts for the girls and if Mac was really looking forward to seeing him. They had barely spoken over the years and when they did, it was awkward. Not the kind of conversations a dad should have with his only son. Dad could be so straightforward when he wanted something to happen and my brother is oddly just like him. He dug his heels in and refused to come home and take over Dad's business. He loved Amy and he did whatever he had to in order to be near her. I was probably kind of jealous of him in that respect because he had the guts to say no and to know that wasn't the route for him to take, but all that was water under the bridge. Anyway, we were all going to be together again at the shore for the first time in a very long time. It had changed me and it had changed Dad, maybe it would change them too.

CHAPTER 44

I woke up early, made my coffee and eased up the steps to Mom's room. I found an old art tablet and some pencils and sat down in the chair to see what I could come up with for the office space. I wanted to give it to Kyle today so I could spend the rest of the time enjoying my family and getting ready for Christmas.

I scribbled a rough drawing of the room's windows and doors so that I could get my bearings. I used my computer to print out different furniture pieces and a paint color chart that mom had to pick out colors. I put it all together and had a very rough idea board to show to him. I used shades of blue like the water with white cotton draperies, neutral furniture and pops of color with pillows and a beautiful rug that was online to pull it all together.

I was kind of embarrassed to show him something so simple but he had always encouraged me and I knew he would never make fun of me, so I figured I would give it a shot. He got there about ten and finished one last small project in the kitchen. I nervously pulled out the idea board to give to him.

"Okay, it's really rough and don't make fun of me," I started before I even let him see it.

He didn't even look at it before he hugged me and said, "Look, you don't need to convince me that you have a gift. I already know it. Hopefully this will convince you."

I nodded and he picked up the board to check it out. He loved the colors, the modern furniture and the fabric blinds that would filter the sun but not hide the view of the marina.

"I love it, Sammy. Can I take this with me?"

"Yea, sure. I mean it's just thrown together with stuff I had here, so it's not fancy or anything. But I guess you get the idea."

"Oh, I get it. It looks great."

Lizzy called to say she was almost there, so Kyle left to head home. He wanted to give us some time together alone without her having to see him again right when she got there. Lizzy, like the rest of my family, loved Kyle. She was younger so he was always teasing her. He taught her how to surf and never cared if she wanted to tag along with us. She would be happy to see him and even happier to see us together. I couldn't wait!

"SAMMY!" She yelled as she jumped out of the car.

"Hey Little Sister!" I ran out to give her a hug. "Did you have a good trip?"

"Yes I did! Long, but good."

"I'm so glad you're here. I have a million things to tell you." I said.

She stopped to look around. Gosh it's literally been forever since I have been here. So many memories, but it still looks about the same. The beach is just as beautiful as ever and look at that water. We headed into the screened porch.

"Dad," I yelled, "Lizzy's here!"

"Where's my Lizzy?" Dad yelled from inside. He came rushing out on to the porch. "Hi honey, it's been too too long," He said squeezing her tight.

"Hey Dad, how have you been? Sammy taking good care of you?"

"She does alright," he teased. "Just look at you! You look great and just as pretty as ever."

Lizzy was beautiful, with her long hair and blue eyes. We actually looked a lot alike since we had gotten older, but Lizzy knew how to enhance her beauty. She knew the right makeup and clothes to wear. She had thought about a modeling career at one point. She never finished college, because she met her husband and he made enough money for her to stay home and college was never her dream.

"Let's go inside out of the cold and get you settled in" I said. "You'll be staying with me."

"You and I sharing a room? Just like old times."

We went inside and I thought she was going to cry.

"Oh my goodness, it's like walking back in time." She laughed, wiping tears off her face. "It's like Mom should me coming down the stairs with some seashell in her hand." We all laughed.

We took her things to my room and got her settled. Then she visited with dad on the porch for a while.

"Want to go to the beach for a walk?"

"Sure, let me grab my coat"

We took off down to the beach like two teenagers. When we used to come in the summer, we would all get there, jump out of the car, throw our stuff in our rooms and run out the door toward the water before Mom could stop us. Every summer was just like the first time we had ever been there. We walked and talked and I filled her in about all the details from Mac and Amy coming Christmas Eve to Dad wanting to move, the shelter and all about me and Kyle. I told her I wanted to show her Mom's room and how it had all been locked up all these years. She was amazed at everything that was happening.

"Sammy, you're different here. You're so relaxed, and so excited about what's happening. I love to see you like this. When am I going to see that good looking boyfriend of yours?"

"Boyfriend? I don't know about that, but he is good looking, very good looking!"

We both laughed.

We walked so far and it was getting colder so we headed back, arm in arm all the way down the beach. I felt like I had so much to cram into the short amount of time that I had with her. I showed her mom's room and all her things and told her about the journal. She sat down in mom's chair and wrapped the blanket around her. She started to cry.

"Lizzy don't cry. I didn't mean to make you sad."

"You didn't make me sad, Sammy, I'm just sad on my own. I think my marriage is falling apart. I won't even be with Scott for Christmas, and I miss Mom. I miss her so much. You're right though, all this makes her feel so close."

"Wait right here just a minute." I ran downstairs and grabbed the journal.

"Here, read this. Read your letter from her. Just take a few minutes to take it all in and I will be downstairs when you get ready to come down."

When Mom died, we all went to the funeral, spent the evening together and then everyone went back home and left Dad and I there alone. I'm not sure any of us ever grieved the way we needed to. I just wanted to give her that time. The time to realize, Mom wasn't gone. She was with us in every sunset, every ocean wave, and every good thing she had given us.

CHAPTER 45

Kyle came back for dinner and brought us pizza. He knocked and opened the door and Sal came busting in and ran right to Lizzy to bark and welcome her.

"Sally Dog! Oh my gosh, I can't believe it." She kneeled down to hug her." And there's that handsome Kyle Martin. My goodness I don't think you have changed one bit!"

"How in the world are you, Lizzy? It's been too long. You look great, but I have to say you're looking more and more like your sister!"

"I will take that as a compliment!" She said.

"That's just how I meant it." He winked.

She turned to me, "Sammy, no wonder you never got over this boy! I was too young to realize what a great guy he was."

My face turned red, "He definitely is, Lizzy."

"Are ya'll gonna talk all night or eat pizza?" Dad said. "I'm starving! Lizzy, they don't ever feed me!"

"I doubt that's true" Lizzy said.

We ate until we were stuffed and then grabbed some ice cream for dessert and headed for the living room. Kyle had the fire burning and we spent the next few hours just catching up and visiting. It was great, just like old times. We only had a couple of days before the Carnival and I wanted to soak up every minute with Lizzy. Kyle left with a promise to show Lizzy around town the next day and dad was fighting to stay awake in his chair. Lizzy was tired from the trip, so we decided to call it a night.

We put on our pajamas and climbed into bed, something we hadn't done since I became a teenager and decided I was too old to share a room with my little sister. We laughed and talked for another hour until Lizzy couldn't hold her eyes open anymore.

I took out my journal and began to write about the building, Lizzy, and how I looked forward to the rest of the week. Finally I turned out the light and lay there in the dark listening to the waves in the distance and wondering what it would be like to be Kyle's wife and live in that pretty little bungalow. I was beginning to see it as a possibility.

CHAPTER 46

I was an early riser, especially at the beach. I always had been, but Lizzy could sleep well into the afternoon. She loved to sleep in. I eased out of the bed and stepped into the bathroom to get dressed and brush my teeth. I wanted to get my walk in before everyone started making plans. My coffee and I headed to the beach. I ran into Mr. Sargent, *aka Santa Clause*, again and he was excited to start the fund raiser the next day. Other than that, there was no one else on the beach to be seen in either direction...just the way I liked it. I walked down to the old tree and found my spot to sit. I think that this was the only place that I had ever been where my brain actually stopped thinking a million things and just allowed me to sit peacefully without worrying or planning or stressing. It was unusually cold though, so I had to cut my time short. I couldn't stand to stay out any longer.

Surprisingly, Lizzy was up and making coffee when I got back. Maybe she rested better at the beach too.

"I don't believe my eyes! Lizzy is up before lunch time? It's actually early!"

She laughed, "Hey, I'm a grown up now too, you know!"

"I hope you're grown up enough to make good coffee," I teased.

"I got this," She said.

We ate some breakfast and got ready to go with Kyle. Dad was coming along for the ride. Kyle took us all around the town and showed Lizzy the things that had changed and the things that remained pretty much the same. We went by Kyle's house and Lizzy fell in love with it as much as I did. We decided to stop at Riley's for a burger. Lizzy was thrilled to see Mrs. Riley. She had been friends with her daughter Carmen when they were younger. Mrs. Riley saw her as soon as we walked in, and came over to hug her.

"Lizzy Alexander, are my eyes playing tricks on me? I can't believe it!"

"Hi Mrs. Riley! How are you doing?" Lizzy asked. "How's Carmen, does she still live here in town?"

"I am just great. How is my Lizzy?"

"I'm good. Man, this place sure brings back some fun memories. I think I spent more time here in the summer than I did at the beach." She laughed.

I could sit at the beach all day, but not Lizzy. She was always looking for something else to do. She and Carmen were inseparable in the summer. They were either at Riley's or the ice cream shop or riding bikes or sitting on the porch making jewelry with mom.

We sat down and ordered lunch and Lizzy and Mrs. Riley caught up about Carmen. She still lived nearby and would be visiting for Christmas and planned to try to make it to the Carnival. Lizzy hoped to get to see her while she was there.

We took her to the shelter to see the photos of mom and meet Dr. Jane and everything we were doing for the fund raiser. She was excited to be there to help us. Tomorrow was the first day of the Christmas Carnival but people were already getting things ready and the company with the rides were already setting them up. We were going to be busy all day long. The carnival didn't start until three o'clock but we had to be there early to get ready. Lizzy agreed to be in charge of taking the photos with Santa and Mrs. Clause. Kyle and I would be in charge of selling the items and Dad would just be helping out. We got back to the house and put together a plan for the next day while we ate dinner that Lizzy and I had made. Tomorrow was going to be a big day. I hoped that we could make my Mom's dream of helping the shelter and the animals come true.

CHAPTER 47

Kyle got there early so we could load everything into his truck. We had planned to grab breakfast on the way, but I couldn't sleep so I had it ready by the time Kyle got there to get us. We drank enough coffee to wake us up and started loading his truck. When everything was loaded, we stopped long enough to eat breakfast. Lizzy asked Kyle about his parents and how they were doing and if they would come to the carnival. He said they usually show up for the food at some point.

"There's going to be food?" Lizzy was excited, "Carnival food?"

"Well yea, it's just like a regular carnival, just with a Christmas theme." Kyle explained. "It has rides and everything. I'm planning to put Sammy on the ferris wheel."

"Oh no, I don't think so. I know you didn't forget that I hate those things."

"Come on Sammy, don't be a chicken!" He and Lizzy started making chicken noises.

"Alright you two ten year olds, I'm not going to be pressured by your chicken noises." I laughed.

"We'll see." Kyle said. "She will be on it before the day is over."

"Bet she won't," Lizzy said.

"How much," Kyle answered.

"Think I might get in on that action." Dad joined in.

"Okay, I'm standing right here! Just talk about me!

I threw the dish towel at them and told them to get their coats on. We had to get started because we had no idea how long it would take. I was hoping that we had it all ready by lunch and could relax for the rest of the afternoon, but there was no way to know so we had to go early. Lizzy drove dad so that we could have two cars there in case we needed it.

By the time we got there the place was crawling with people. I was surprised to see that it looked like the entire town was there setting up. We found our assigned booth, which was in a great location to have all the dogs. It was at the end of the row near a grassy area, so we had plenty of space. We got out and unloaded the truck and started figuring out where it would all go. We worked so hard, but when we were finished, our booth looked awesome. We had an area for Santa and Mrs. Clause, an area for the pets that needed adoption and an area for all the merchandise. We had a banner that read "Paw Pics with Santa for the Pier City Animal Shelter." It looked great.

Dr. Jane was bringing some of the dogs and cats over later before it started and then she would go back and get more as some were adopted. I really hoped this went well. None of us had ever done anything like this before, but we gave it our all. Even Sal was helping. We made her a sign to wear across her back that said. "Adopt my friends, they need a home for Christmas."

We worked straight through lunch and were finishing up just as it was almost time to start. The mayor counted down and when he got to One everyone shouted Merry Christmas! Whoever had built the booths had put Christmas lights on each one, so they all came on at once. The carnival rides lit up and

Christmas music began to play and people began to pour onto the street with the booths.

We were crazy busy and it was crazy fun. We took turns getting our favorite foods when there was a lull in the crowd. It seemed like the entire county brought their pets to be photographed with Santa and while they were waiting in line, they bought collars and treats, and toys. I never imagined that it would go so well.

Kyle and I took a break together and grabbed some food at one of the trucks.

"Let's go, Sammy, time to conquer that fear and help me win that bet."

"Ugh, you know I hate those things."

"I know you do, but I will never let anything happen to you and I want you to see all these lights from up there. Pleeeaase?"

"Well since you said please, but I swear if you rock that seat one single time, I will kill you!"

"No rocking, you have my word."

We got on the ferris wheel and it slowly climbed upward, stopping every two minutes to let someone on. We finally got to the top and stopped. I hated just hanging there. I didn't mind the going around, but hanging there was awful.

"Oh gosh, I hate this," I closed my eyes and buried my head into Kyle's chest.

"Sammy, you have to look. Open your eyes. You're going to miss it!" He took my face in his hand and turned it so I could see.

"Open your eyes. I promise you will be glad."

I slowly opened my eyes and looked at him, then looked down at the carnival. It was so pretty. The sun was starting to go down with all its colors behind the rides that were lit up and twirling and spinning. All the little booths were lit up with the Christmas lights. He was right it was worth it and he didn't rock the seat one time. The ride started to go around. He put his arm around me and pulled me close. We laughed until there were cold tears on our faces. I felt like I was eighteen again. When the ride was over, we headed back to give Dad and Lizzy a break.

By the end of the night, we were all exhausted. Even Sal was trying to take a nap. We pulled a big tarp down over our booth, thanked Santa and Mrs. Clause and headed home with the little metal box full of money. We were frozen to the bone, so Kyle built a fire as soon as we got inside.

Finally, what we had waited for all day long, we opened the box on the bar and dumped the money onto the counter. We each started separating the bills so we could count them. After all was said and done, we had made over fifteen hundred dollars that evening and had four dogs and three cats adopted. I was happy because I never imagined we would have such a successful night. We counted out the money for the change we needed for the next day and put the rest in a locked bank bag and put it in the closet for safe keeping. We should have been falling over from exhaustion, but we were too excited. We sat and talked for another hour. We were really doing it, our plan was working!

That night, as I fell asleep, I kept hearing Kyle's words in my head. "Open your eyes, Sammy, you're going to miss how great this is."

I didn't want to miss a single thing. I was becoming brave because of him. I was having the courage to open my eyes and my heart.

CHAPTER 48

Today would be another full day. We didn't have to be there quite as early, but we did need to straighten things back up and get ready to open. I tried to get Dad to stay home where it was warm, but he would not hear of it. He wanted to be right in the middle of everything that was going on.

We were almost ready to open when someone walked up to the booth.

"Lizzy Alexander, how long has it been?"

"Oh my gosh, Carmen! I can't believe it's really you. I never thought I would see you again!" Lizzy grabbed her and hugged her tight. She stepped back and looked at her and then grabbed her again.

"Mom said your family was here, and I just had to see you! How are you?"

"I'm good. Gosh it's so great to see your face again. All of my memories of this place involve you."

"We have to catch up before you leave." Carmen said.

"Are you going to be here all evening? Come back in about an hour and I will be able to go somewhere and sit down for a little bit." Lizzy asked.

"Ok sounds great. See you then!" Lizzy couldn't believe she actually got to see her again.

"Can you believe that?' She said, "She looks amazing. We had so much fun in those summers. You know, I never had a friend at home as good as her. She was always my best friend. We wrote to each other for a long time after we stopped coming to the beach, but we both kind of drifted apart as we got older. It really makes me miss this place. Do you think you and dad will move here, Sammy?"

"I don't know what I will do, Lizzy." I answered.

Kyle had gone to get us some hot chocolate so it was just the two of us. "I really want to be with Kyle. Honestly I don't think that I ever stopped loving him and being with him feels so right."

"Yea, I can tell. You guys seem happier than ever."

"But Howard called and said I really need to be back right after Christmas. How will I explain to Kyle that I have to leave? I don't want to hurt him again."

"Not much to explain I guess." Kyle had walked back up to the booth. "I get it Sammy, but you could have said something to my face. Wait, that's how you do it, right? You just make plans and leave without telling anyone."

"Kyle, that's not what I was say...."

"Look, you don't owe me an explanation, I knew I was taking a chance when I hung out with you the first time. I get it. Listen, I'm going to call it a night. I hope you guys are able to sell everything. I can take the rest to the shelter when the carnival is over. Come on Sal, let's go home."

"Kyle, wait, please let me explain."

"Like I said, no explanation needed."

He got in his truck and backed out and left me standing there. I looked at Lizzy with tears in my eyes.

"What just happened?"

"Sammy, maybe he just needs some space. Surely he will give you a chance to explain. Maybe he's just so scared of it happening that he jumped to conclusions when he heard you say that."

"Yea, you think? He could have at least let me explain before he just leaves. Besides we needed his help tonight, and he just walked away without so much as even thinking about that.

People started walking up and dad came back from seeing Mrs. Riley.

"Dad we need your help tonight." Lizzy said. "Kyle went home."

"What? Why, is he sick?"

I didn't even answer, but Lizzy told him what happened.

"Let him cool off, Sammy. That's boy cares too much about you to just walk away."

"Whatever Dad," I acted like I didn't care, but I was heartbroken. How could he just leave me standing there because of what he thought he heard?

Fortunately we were so busy, I didn't have much time to worry about it. I felt sick to my stomach all night. I didn't know if I would get a chance to even tell him what had happened. We had a great night and somehow managed for Lizzy to get to visit with Carmen too. Finally it was time to head home. I sat in silence as Lizzy drove us home.

CHAPTER 49

I walked into the house and went straight to the shower, washed my hair and got in bed. I checked my phone, but there was no missed call or text message. I took out my journal and read the previous pages about all the fun we had been having. Then I added a page about tonight. Somehow writing it all down like a prayer made me feel better and not so worried but I still tossed and turned all night long and woke up with the sun. Lizzy must have slept in the living room to give me some privacy because she wasn't in the bed when I woke up. I had to go to the beach for a walk. The sun had not even finished rising as I headed out the door with my coffee. My head was spinning. I wanted to cry and scream. Did he not know by now that I wanted to be there with him? Had I not made it clear?

I had never come right out and said it, but he should know. Shouldn't he?

How would he know, I had already left him once before and I changed the subject every time he mentioned anything about a future but it wasn't because I didn't want a future. I was just weird and awkward.

I was so confused. I felt like I had come full circle and was reliving my past all over again. All the heartache, tears and confusion were right back in my face. I wanted to run. I could just leave and never look back. Just repeat the entire thing again. I survived the first time, except this time, I did already have a job and a home of my own. I had only been back a month, it would surely be easier.

I made it to the tree where I normally sit and I just sat there and sobbed. I had all these answers to my two lives swirling around in my head, but since he left, maybe the decision had already been made for me. When I had no tears left, I headed back toward the house with no answers, but I had plenty to do. That's what I do, I do stuff. I stay busy. I don't deal with things, I work. It was Christmas Eve. The rest of my family would be there soon, and we had one remaining evening left at the carnival. I still didn't even know how much money we had made. I had to focus and pull myself together. By the time I got back to the house, Dad was on the porch swing having his coffee.

"Morning Dad," I said casually.

"Morning Honey, are you okay?"

"I don't know, I guess I have to be okay don't I?"

"Sammy, what in the world happened? Come here and sit down for a minute."

I walked over and sat down and dad put his arm around me. I started to cry again.

"I don't know Dad. He heard me talking to Lizzy about going home and how Howard had called and said I needed to get back right after Christmas, but he didn't hear the whole conversation. I also said I thought I was in love with him and I wanted to stay here."

"Well, what are you going to do about it?"

"I don't know Dad. We have a business and I can't just pack a suitcase and leave all those people there working with no boss. I have responsibilities. You have another house there full of all your things. We can't just pretend all those things don't exist."

"What do you want to do, Sammy? What do you really want to do if you didn't have those things going on?"

"I would come here and live and walk on the beach every single day with Kyle. I would help him with remodels on businesses and houses. I just love it, Dad. But I do have all those things going on, and now he won't even speak to me."

"It will work out somehow, honey. Sometimes you just have to follow your heart and take a giant leap of faith and see where you land. I know you, and you will land on your feet and be just great!" He kissed me on the head.

"I hope so Dad, I really hope so." But I wasn't sure I even knew what he meant about leaps of faith. I did everything with a plan, remember?

I went inside to find Lizzy counting the money from the night before. The carnival was only in the evening today, so we didn't have to be there so early.

We made another eighteen hundred dollars and had six more dogs and cats adopted. I was so glad it was going well, but now I was tired and I just wanted to curl up in bed and cry. Everything was such a mess. I hadn't meant for Kyle to think I was just going to leave him again. I had been so back and forth whenever the subject got brought up, I could see how he could have doubts.

Mac said he and Amy and the girls would be there before the carnival that afternoon. I knew I had to get a shower and get myself straightened up before they arrived. I wanted the girls to have a great time. I never got to see them and I sure didn't want them to see me all weepy and sad. Lizzy asked if I was okay and if she could help me do anything, but I just didn't want to talk about it anymore. She looked like she had been crying too and I almost didn't even notice.

"Are you okay? You look upset about something yourself?"

"Yea, I'm okay I guess except that it's Christmas Eve and my husband is in another state not even answering my calls."

"Lizzy, I'm sorry. I was so caught up in myself, I didn't even realize you were upset. It will be okay because the Alexanders are all going to be together and we are going to have a great Christmas." I tried to sound cheerful. "And I can't wait to see those girls having fun at that carnival."

"You're right," She agreed, "Let's get moving and get our minds onto something else.

My mind couldn't think of anything but Kyle's face from the night before. I had to just make myself go through the motions. I should be good at it by now.

CHAPTER 50

We got to the carnival a little earlier to straighten up. It was shorter because it was Christmas Eve and many people would be home with their families, but they still wanted to have it for the people just getting into town. They had just started the countdown to open up when we finished straightening our last shelf. Dr. Jane was there to help and two other girls, so Lizzy and I could enjoy some time with our family. I could hardly even focus for looking around to see if I saw Kyle. I knew him well enough to know that he wouldn't be there, unless he came to see me. He wouldn't just show up and walk around.

We were busy right off the bat. I didn't know how there were any people left that had not already had their picture with Santa, but there was a line out of our booth and down the aisle. I was right in the middle of talking to a customer when I heard someone yell at me.

"Hey! Has anyone seen my little sisters?" It was Mac!

Lizzy and I both dropped what we were doing and ran out to hug him!

"Look at you two," He said. "It's been too long." He
hugged us tight while Amy and the girls looked on. We finally got
loose and ran to hug them. The girls had grown so tall and were
both so pretty.

"Amy! You look so great! I'm so glad ya'll made it. Girls, we
are going to have so much fun this weekend." They smiled shyly.

Dad was coming out of the booth when the girls saw him.

"Pop," They yelled and ran to see him. The almost ran him
over in their excitement.

"Girls, slow down. You don't want to knock Pop over, do
you?" Mac came up behind them.

"Hey son, how are you?" Dad said, awkwardly.

"I'm okay, Dad. How about yourself?"

"Doing pretty good. I've missed you!" They grabbed each
other and embraced for the first time in years. I thought we were
all going to cry. The girls interrupted because they caught site of
one of the puppies in the cages.

"Mom, look at the puppy! You know I want a puppy for
Christmas! I already asked Santa."

"Sara, you know we have talked about this. We just don't
have time for a dog, but you can go pet it if you want."

We stood there and talked for a few minutes and Dr. Jane
interrupted and told us to go have some fun and she and her girls
would watch the booth for a while.

"Sara, Sally, you want to go get some food and ride some
rides?" I yelled.

They both came running, but Sara assured the puppy that
she would be back soon.

We spent the next two hours eating, and laughing and
taking turns riding things with the girls. They figured out that all
they had to do was look at their Pop with their sweet faces and he
would hand over more money for tickets. He was having a blast
with them. It gave us a chance to catch up with Mac and Amy. He
immediately wanted to know where Kyle and Lizzy's husband,
Chris, were at.

She told him he was working and I just gave him a quick run-down of what had happened with Kyle. We told him not to worry about us and that we just wanted to have fun visiting with them, but he could tell we were still upset.

He laughed, "I don't think I have ever seen our dad hand out money so freely. Dad, be careful, they will break you before you know it."

"Shoot, I'm having the time of my life. Worth every penny!

Mac looked at me confused, "You're right. Our father was abducted by aliens and it has changed him." We all laughed.

Dad didn't care that we were teasing him. He was just trying to keep up with two little girls that were running him from booth to booth. Before long, they were all three tired and the girls wanted to go back and see the puppy. We all went back to the booth. It wouldn't be open much longer, then we would head to the house. I told the girls that I had a surprise for them there. They couldn't wait. I had hoped Kyle and I could show them the bunks together, but that wasn't going to happen.

The night came to a close and the crowds dwindled. We hardly had any merchandise left, so Dr. Jane put it in her truck. The only puppy left was the one the girls had been playing with. They were heartbroken to have to leave it, but I talked them into riding with me home so we could talk about what Santa was bringing them that night. Mac and Amy had brought most of their gifts along in a carrier on top of the van, but the girls had no idea and they weren't sure Santa could find them at a new house. By the time they got to the house, they had forgotten about the puppy. Mac and Amy took longer to get back than us. I asked them if they had gotten lost.

The girls had never been to the beach house, so they were beyond excited. I made them close their eyes before I showed them the beds. I counted to three and they opened their eyes. The both screamed happy screams and jumped on the beds. We decided that they could take turns sleeping on the top bunk. They wanted to read all the books that night. We turned on the tree lights and built a fire and roasted marshmallows with them. They had a long trip and before long they were both on Dad's lap in his chair and all three were sound asleep. Mac carried them to their beds and tucked them in. He looked around the house and commented about how it still looked and felt the same. It felt good to be back. Then he said he had a surprise in the car and needed to go get it.

"Look what I got," He whispered. He pulled his jacket back and was holding the tiny white puppy the girls had been playing with. It was sound asleep too.

"You got it?" Lizzy said loudly and then caught herself and clasped her hands over her mouth.

Mac and Amy were laughing. We had planned to get them one this year, but we couldn't figure out how to do it with making this trip.

"They are going to just die." I said, "Get ready for the girl screams!"

"Oh we are well acquainted with girl screams, trust me." Amy said. "But we have to find a way to keep him quiet until morning."

"We can put the kennel in our room in the closet. It's empty except for a few clothes and our suitcases. He will probably sleep all night."

We sat out all the presents, and hugged each other goodnight. It was so odd, but so great to be back together in this house again with all my people. Mom would have loved this so much. I thought Dad might cry when he told us goodnight.

"I'm just so glad for us all to be here together. Thank you all for making this happen. It's the best Christmas present I have ever gotten.

CHAPTER 51

I wasn't happy that it was Christmas Eve and I was alone again. I had spent so many Christmases alone and I thought for sure this one was going to be different. I missed Kyle so much and I wondered what he was doing. Was he home alone with just Sal to keep him company? Would he wake up in the morning alone? I had tried to call him once, but he didn't answer or call me back so I figured he didn't want to talk to me. Lizzy tried again to call Chris, but still no answer. She didn't seem worried, only sad. This had been the best month of my life, how could it be ending like this?

The puppy whined half the night until finally I tucked it in between me and Lizzy and it fell sound asleep. I guess it was feeling kind of lonely too, but in the morning it was going to be one happy little dog. She reminded me of Sal when Kyle and I first got her. She was so little he could hold her in his hand. Every memory I had of Kyle was a good one, how could I hurt him again like this? I finally drifted off to sleep and woke to the sun coming through the window. I quietly went out the front door and took the tiny puppy outside to pee. It was freezing! Colder than it had been the entire time I had been here and the sky was white with low hanging clouds. I hurried back inside without waking the girls and put the puppy back in bed with Lizzy.

As soon as the coffee pot began to drip, they were awake and remembered what day it was. They both jumped up and out of the beds and ran to the Christmas tree. There were so many gifts they spread out into the floor. They started picking up boxes and shaking them to see if they could tell what was inside.

"You two better go get your mom and dad up and Pop before you start messing with the presents," I said. That was all the permission they needed to run down the hall yelling for them to wake up.

"Merry Christmas, Pop!" They yelled as they both jumped on Dad's bed. "Wake up! We have to open presents!"

"Presents? Someone got presents?" Dad teased. "Did I get a present?"

"Let's go see, Pop! Get up!" They were pulling him out of the bed while he was trying to grab his robe. He came down the hall with a little girl on each side holding his hands, smiling from ear to ear. By the time they got back in there, Mac and Amy were up getting coffee and finding a seat. Lizzy came wondering out of the bedroom still in a daze. We let the girls open all of their gifts and then Mac snuck into the bedroom to get the puppy.

"Girls I think Santa left one more present!" They both stopped what they were doing and looked up. He pulled the puppy out from his robe.

"I think he thought you girls might like this little girl to be your friend and go home with you."

Sara burst into tears and Sally just jumped up and down over and over. It brought tears to all of our eyes to see them so excited. They gently took the puppy and sat here down between them.

"Is she really ours to keep, Dad?" Sara asked with her big blue eyes looking up at Mac.

"For keeps?" Sally chimed in.

"Yep, she is all yours to keep, but you have to learn how to take care of her. She is like a baby and puppies need lots of love and attention." He said.

All the other presents took a backseat to this and they were enthralled by every move she made. While they were playing, we exchanged our gifts with each other and with dad. Lizzy gave me a gorgeous locket and Mac and Amy gave me a gold bracelet and earrings to match. I gave each of them the letters that mom had written in a frame. I had taken them and had them matted and placed in nice frames to keep them from aging. I gave dad one of her paintings. It was a picture of the beach with the shape of a couple walking. He opened it and just stared at it. It was like having her in the room with us. We all sat there quietly until Dad spoke.

"Guys, I just want you to know that having you here together is the most special gift any of you could have given me. We have spent so many fun times here and I wish I would have been here for more of those fun times. I had my priorities all confused and now I am an old man, but I love you all and I want to have more times like this so I am going to make some changes in my life."

We just listened without saying a word, each of us wiping tears from our eyes.

"Over the years, I worked hard and made good money and I invested that money wisely. Your mother and I talked about doing this many times and I know this is what she would want too. Let me finish before you say anything please. Sammy, as you know, I want to live here now, but when I am gone, this house will be yours. You love it here like your mother did and she always wanted you to have it because she knew you would be the one to treasure it most."

"Dad!"

"Now wait, please, like I asked," He continued quietly. Lizzy, our other house now belongs to you. When I get my stuff out of it, you can live there or sell it or whatever you like, it's yours. You loved living there in that town more than any of us did and that was always home to you. And Mac, because of the investments I have made, I would like to give you and Amy the money to pay off your mortgage and you won't have to worry about that hanging over your head."

We were stunned. We didn't know what to say or where to begin. How could he do that?

"And I have one more thing to announce, I have talked with some business people and some of my old partners and if Sammy is ready to make the move, then I want to sell the firm. She has worked hard to take care of it and get it to where it is at and so if she is ready to go a different direction, then I am ready for her to, but if she decides to stay, then it will remain in the family. If we sell, then she and I will each take thirty-five percent of the profit and Lizzy you and Mac will each get fifteen percent. I feel like that is fair because Sammy literally left her life to run that business. I will live off my percentage, then when I am gone, you all will split what is left evenly. It will take a little while to take care of all the details, but that's what I want to happen. Your mother and I always knew that we wanted to get to see you enjoy the inheritance that we had for you all."

He continued, "Sammy, I have talked to Howard and he has met with the top people in the firm, and they believe that they can run it if you want to only work a few hours a week from here, just so you can stay on top of things until the sell is final and you will still get your salary."

Mac spoke first," Dad this is a lot to wrap our heads around. Are you sure you want to live here and are you sure Sammy wants to make a move like that?"

"I believe she does." He said, looking at me. I nodded and burst into tears. I felt like a million pounds had been lifted off my shoulders.

"I didn't realize how much I wasn't living being at that office every day, Mac. I don't know what I will do, but I belong here at the shore."

"And Mac, I just want you to know, I'm proud of you son. I'm proud that you stood up for yourself years ago and went after the life you wanted with Amy. I wish I could have seen it sooner. I'm sorry, son. You're a great man and a great father!" Dad said. They grabbed each other and hugged for what seemed like forever. We were all crying and laughing and hugging each other. We were a family again. Then someone knocked on the door.

CHAPTER 52

One of the girls ran to the door to open it. There stood Chris. Lizzy jumped up from the couch and ran to the door. Chris was one of the sweetest people you ever met. He was so thoughtful of everyone and loved Lizzy to death. I guess he had just gotten his priorities out of order. I could relate, for sure.

"What on earth are you doing here," She asked. "I have been calling you since yesterday."

"I know, but I wanted to surprise you and I knew if I answered, I would end up telling you before I could get here. I didn't want to spend Christmas without you. I love you, and I'm sorry I have been taking you for granted."

Lizzy was in shock. She gave him a huge kiss and we all laughed.

I could hardly believe what was happening. Was I actually going to live here? This was my house? That was my room upstairs. It couldn't be possible. What would Kyle think? Would he even care at this point? I turned around and watched my family embracing and laughing with each other and I had to look toward heaven because I knew my Mom was busy again.

We laughed and talked all morning. Then we all bundled up and took the puppy down to the beach for a walk. It was great even though it was very cold. The girls chased the puppy and then it chased them. Mac and Amy held hands and walked along the water like they used to and Lizzy was showing Chris every detail of the beach.

"It's been a great day, Dad. You had a very good Idea." I said as I looped my arm through his.

"Yea I came up with a pretty good one this time, "He laughed, "Your mother would have been proud of me. But I couldn't have done any of this without you, Sammy. You have been the one that made all this happen. You have worked so hard and sacrificed so much. Now it's your turn to be happy."

"Yea I'm not sure how well that's gonna turn out, Dad, but we will see."

"What's there to see about?"

"My happiness involves Kyle and I don't even know what he is thinking right now."

"Why don't you ask him?"

"Maybe, if I get another chance I will." I said.

"Maybe you have a chance right now," He motioned up the beach and Sal was running to me full speed. Kyle was about a hundred feet behind him running through the sand. I turned and started walking toward him. I had never been so happy to see someone in my entire life. Sal got to me first and jumped up with both sandy paws and knocked me off my feet. I couldn't help but laugh.

Kyle was standing over me offering his hand to help me to my feet. I couldn't believe he was actually there. I looked up at him and gave him my hand. He helped me up and held on to it.

"Sammy, I just had to see you today and talk to you."

"I wanted to talk to you too. I'm so sorry about..."

"Wait, let me go first," He said. "When we started hanging out again, I told you I didn't have any expectations and if I only got to spend a month with you it would be worth it to me to take the chance on you leaving again. But when I heard you say something about going home, it brought back all the pain from last time and the fear of losing you again and I just reacted. I'm so sorry. I want you to be happy and that's all and if that means leaving me to go back to your job and home, then that's what you should do. I want you to be free to do what is important to you. I love you Sammy, and I never stopped loving you and I want you to be happy with your life."

He just stood there holding my hand waiting on me to speak.

"Kyle, I love you too and the only way I can be happy is to be with you, and to be here at the shore. I'm not going back. This is my home, this is where my heart lives, you are where my heart is and I could never be happy anywhere else."

"You're staying here? At the beach? To live? How?"

"Yes, you're stuck with me I'm afraid and it's a long story combined with a Christmas gift."

"Did ya'll hear that?" He screamed as loud as he could. "She's staying here with me! She'll be living right here in this town with me! Woohoo!!" He grabbed me and picked me up and swung me around. He kissed me and yelled again!

Sal was barking and everyone came running. Kyle grabbed my dad and hugged him.

"I know you had something to do with this and I could never thank you enough."

"Well, you will be stuck with me too," Dad laughed. "I guess we're a package deal!"

"That's alright too," Kyle said. Then he saw Mac and Amy and reached to hug them both. "Mac, Amy, how in the world are you? So good to see you!"

We all just stood in the freezing cold talking and laughing and watching Sal meet the new puppy, when all of the sudden a light flurry of snow started falling. We thought we were seeing things at first, but then the flakes got a little bigger.

"It's snowing," I screamed, "The one thing I wanted to see for Christmas. It's snowing on the beach!"

"I can't believe it really is snowing, Kyle said. It hasn't snowed here in years."

The girls were running and trying to catch snowflakes on their tongues. The flakes got bigger until it started falling steadily on the sand. People all down the beach were coming out to see.

"Merry Christmas, Sammy," Kyle whispered. "I love you so much. This is the best Christmas I have ever had."

"Merry Christmas," I said as I snuggled close to him. "I have never been happier."

"Are you guys ready for some brunch and to start Christmas dinner before we starve?" Lizzy asked.

Mac laughed, "Leave it to Lizzy to remember the food."

We headed into the house to get warm, when Kyle stopped.

"Oh yea, I had something else to tell you. You know the client with the business office? He loved your ideas and wants you to be the designer of the space."

"Oh my gosh, you have got to be kidding," I said.

"Nope, that space and several others he has here and in the next town over."

I couldn't believe it. I might actually have the opportunity to do what I wanted. This day started out so horrible and had completely turned around. I didn't think it could get any better. Sometimes you just have to wait for things to float to the surface, right Mom?

CHAPTER 53

We told Dr. Jane that we would meet her at the shelter after the girls opened gifts and we had breakfast. We wanted to take her all the money as a family and Dad had written a check to the shelter and placed it in a card. We loaded everyone into Mac's van and Kyle's truck along with dogs and headed over to the shelter. She was going to be so surprised, but she said she had a surprise for us too. There wasn't enough snow to cover the streets and it was only a few miles to get over there, but the snow was still falling slowly. Kyle still couldn't believe it was snowing.

"You know this snow is like a Christmas miracle right?"

"Yea, I know." I said, "Think my mom is enjoying herself today." I smiled.

"I wanted to donate to the shelter too", Kyle said. "That's where we got Sal, and she has been my best friend since day one."

"What do you want to do?" I asked.

"I would like to bring some equipment in and grade the lot next to the building and pay to have it fenced so the dogs have a big outdoor play area, and maybe plant some trees there for shade in the summer. What do you think?"

"I think that would be awesome and make such a difference for the dogs and maybe even a caged in area for the cats so they can get fresh air too."

"See, those great ideas are why I keep you around." He teased.

Everyone was following us so when we made the turn on the road, Kyle slowed down to wait for them to catch up. We could see the shelter ahead.

"What on earth are they all doing here?" I asked. Dr. Jane and the staff and several volunteers were standing outside in the front yard.

"Maybe they are just watching the snow." I said.

We all pulled in and got out of the car. She hugged us all, but the other people just stood there. "I'm glad you all could come, especially on Christmas Day." She said. "Your mother, Mary, meant so much to me and this shelter and the animals here were so important to her. I want you to know she was such a wonderful woman and she was my friend. What you all have done for this shelter, will mean more than you can ever imagine and I'm so grateful".

At this point, we were all wiping tears from our eyes.

She continued, "Having said all that, I wanted to do something special for you all to show our appreciation."

When she said that, the volunteers separated and we could see a new sign for the shelter. It said The Mary Alexander Animal Shelter.

"We decided in her memory and in appreciation for her heart for this shelter, to rename the shelter in her honor. I hope you will see how much I appreciated her and how much I appreciate you all."

My dad was crying now and all of us were wiping tears off our faces. It was the most special thing she could have done to honor our mother. I squeezed her tightly and held on while we both cried. She hugged each of us, and when she got to Dad she said, "She was a fortunate woman to have you."

He assured her that he was the fortunate one.

We wanted to present her with the money we had earned for the shelter, so we stepped inside.

"Dr. Jane, with all of our hard work, I am very happy to tell you that we were able to earn forty-eight hundred dollars at the carnival to give to the shelter. We hope that will go a long way to help you get the things you need. We got to see about fifteen animals find new homes for Christmas and we really boosted the support of the town."

"Oh my goodness," She said. "I can't believe we made that much. I want to do some improvements around here and that will help so much.

Then Kyle told her his plan to landscape the lot next to the building. She was so excited that the dogs would be able to go out of their cages to run and play outside and they would have room to train them so they would be easier to adopt.

"Last but not least, Dr. Jane," Dad said, "I wanted to make a donation in Mary's name for fifty thousand dollars. Mary would have wanted me to give you this money, and I hope it will go a long way to help the work that you do here."

She just began to cry harder. She grabbed Dad and squeezed him again through her tears.

"I never expected anything like that. Oh my goodness, that's just beyond what I could have imagined." She put her hands over her face and was simply speechless.

It felt like we were somehow able to give our mother a Christmas gift even though she wasn't there with us, not in body anyway. She had devoted her time to this place without ever even telling any of us how much it meant to her. She never bragged on the time that she gave to volunteer and never even told anyone that she spent her summer days coming here just to help in any way she could. That's the way she preferred to do things. She didn't need or want any recognition. Somehow we were able to give her a gift for all that. We hugged everyone and thanked them

again and then headed back to the beach house. Our hearts were
full.

CHAPTER 54

When we got back, everyone went inside to relax and I started on the food for Christmas dinner. I made coffee and hot chocolate and Mac built a fire in the fireplace. I told the girls I had a surprise for them and they came running. I pulled out the Christmas cookies and all the icing and told them they could decorate. Everyone came into the kitchen to join in. It was working. I was able to bring back to life some of the Christmas traditions that we shared as kids. I never knew this would be so important to me. I didn't even like to cook.

After everyone ate cookies to hold them over, they all went to the living room to catch up. Kyle talked to Mac and Amy and got to meet Chris for the first time. They talked about old days at the beach and Mac said that since Dad would be living here now, they would come more often and bring the girls so they could grow up having the wonderful summers that our parents had given us. The girls loved Kyle and asked if he could teach them to surf in the ocean like he had their dad and it wasn't long before he was chasing them through the house with a Nerf gun like a ten year old. That poor puppy just fell asleep from exhaustion.

We all went up to Mom's room and Mac and Amy looked at all her things. I showed the girls how I had made their bracelets with her beads that she had saved and made out of shells. I told them that they were very special and that they should always treasure them. Mac sat down in her chair and told Sara and Sally that this was her special room that she loved to be in and to paint and make things.

When we got back downstairs, Dad was in his chair, the girls were playing in the floor and the puppy was curled up next to Sal asleep.

"Hey, that puppy needs a name," Kyle said. "What are you going to call her?"

"We don't know. What do you think we should call her?" Sally asked.

"Hmmm, let me think," Kyle said. "How about Sandy? She's the color of the sand and you got her at the beach?"

"Yes!" The girls chimed in together.

"Sandy it is then." Mac said.

Sara looked out the window and the snow had started to cover the ground a little bit. "Guys, it's STILL snowing!" She was delighted.

I noticed Kyle's gift was still under the tree. I had completely forgotten to give it to him when we came inside. We were so excited about the snow and each other.

"I forgot to give you your Christmas present," I said.

"You did? You didn't have to get me a present." He said, "I got you." He smiled and kissed me.

"Well, you got a present too!" I said.

"Let's have it then."

I handed him the wrapped gift from under the tree. Everyone stopped to see what it was. I had given him the painting that my mother had painted of Sal when she was a puppy. I had it matted and framed a couple of weeks before. He was blown away.

"Sammy, this is just so special, your mom meant the world to me. Are you sure you don't want to keep it in your family?"

"You meant the world to her and yes I'm sure."

"Well, thank you, I love it" He said. I'm sorry I didn't get you anything.

"Don't be silly," I just saw that upstairs when we first got here and thought you might like it."

"I do. I love it."

CHAPTER 55

Mac decided he would take the puppy and the girls back outside to play a little while before we finished dinner. The snow was still blowing, so they bundled up with hats and gloves I had gotten them for Christmas and headed out the door.

"Hey, Kyle, want to join us? Chris, you want to come down to the beach with us?

Both the guys agreed to go laughing and whispering to each other.

"What are they up to? Acting like teenage boys." I laughed.

"Who knows," Amy said. "Mac is always teasing with the girls about something."

We stayed inside to finish dinner. It was nice to get the time with Lizzy and Amy, but they were being really quiet as we got dinner ready.

Sara and Sally ran onto the screened porch, "Hey everyone, come look at our snowman!"

"Snowman? I don't think it snowed that much already did it?"

We grabbed our coats and hats and headed outside toward the beach. It was still blowing snow and the little bit of sun shining through the clouds was sinking into the water. I could barely see the guys down

232

at the beach and I couldn't figure out what they were doing. When we got closer, Kyle walked up in front of me.

"Close your eyes, I have a surprise for you."

"A surprise? What did you do? You said you didn't get me a present."

"Close your eyes, nosy girl!"

"Okay, okay! They're closed." I said, squeezing my eyes tight.

"You promise?" He said. "They better be closed."

"Yes! They're closed! But I can't see where I'm walking so don't let me go."

After a few steps, we were on the beach because I could only feel the lose sand under my feet. He stepped to my right side and held my hand.

"Can I open my eyes now?" I was so excited. He knew I loved surprises.

"Okay, you can open them now." He said.

I opened my eyes to see jars with candles in them out on the sand. They were so pretty all lit up and my family was standing behind them. My eyes adjusted to the light and I was starting to see better. The jars had candles in them and they were set up on the sand to spell: MARRY ME? What on earth?

When I turned to look at Kyle, he was on one knee beside me. I couldn't speak or believe my eyes. I clasped my hands over my mouth to keep from screaming.

"Sammy Alexander, I have never stopped loving you and I have never loved anyone besides you. You stole my heart so many years ago and I never got it back. The worst times in my life were when I wasn't with you and the happiest day of my life was when you stepped back into it a few weeks ago. I don't ever want to lose you or be apart from you again. It has always been you in my heart and I want to spend the rest of my life until I'm an old, old man showing you that. I want to watch the sunrise and set with you every day. I want to have a family with you and spend my days trying to make you the happiest girl on the planet.

Sammy, will you marry me, will you be mine forever?"

I didn't have to think! For the first time in forever, I didn't have to weigh out both sides of the decision and count the good and bad points. I didn't need a plan or an outline or even to know what the future would hold. I knew the answer beyond the shadow of a doubt.

"YES, YES, YES!! I love you so much, I don't even have words to say how happy I am when I'm with you!" He slid a ring on my finger and kissed me.

He grabbed me and yelled, "SHE SAID YES EVERYBODY!" He swung me around and kissed me again.

They all started clapping and ran to hug and congratulate us. Even Kyle's mom and dad had snuck over to watch. How did he do it? They had all tricked me, but I was too happy to care! This had to be the best day of my life.

We all went inside and all the girls wanted to see my ring. It was so gorgeous. Everyone congratulated us and his mother and father hugged me tight.

"Sammy, we always hoped you would be the girl that Kyle gave this ring to. It was my mother's first ring and mine. I hope you will treasure it and know how happy we are that you will finally be part of this family."

"Thank you Mrs. Martin. That means so much to me." I said.

"No more, Mrs. Martin," She said, "Call me Mom or whatever you like, but not Mrs. Martin!" She laughed and hugged me again. His dad had always loved me and he squeezed me and said, "Welcome to the family, Sammy. I always wanted a daughter."

I was still in shock and all smiles. I just kept staring at my hand and at Kyle.

Even through dinner, I could barely eat. I had butterflies. Was this even real? I just got engaged on Christmas day to the love of my life and I was going to live at the beach. This could not possibly be happening.

It had been a long, wonderful day and I could not have asked for more. After dinner, we all had dessert in the living room and watched the fire and the girls played with Sandy. Kyle's parents left shortly after that and it was just us again.

"So, I got you good," Kyle said.

"Yes, you did! Did all you guys know he was doing this?"

"Well, he had planned it a week ago, but then you had your misunderstanding and we didn't know what was going to happen." Dad said. But He did ask my permission to ask you and I really do appreciate that gesture Kyle. I just want you to know that we all have always loved you like one of our family members and Mary and I always wanted you to be the one for Sammy."

"I'm just glad it all worked out and that you two are finally together and happy." Lizzy said. Then she looked at Kyle, "And you, you better take care of my sister. She is my best friend. I know when we were kids her and Mac left me out, but we aren't kids anymore and she is so important to me."

"You have my word, Sammy." Kyle said and squeezed my hand.

Mac stood up and said, "I would like to say something too."

He never spoke in front of people so, I was caught completely off guard.

"Sammy, seven years ago, you chose to leave this place that you loved and to leave your soul mate to take over a job that I didn't want, just to make sure our parents were taken care of. You buried all your dreams and drove away to do what you thought was the right thing and I want to thank you for that. I also want to tell you how happy I am that you get another chance and that you and Kyle waited for each other without even knowing you were waiting."

By now there wasn't a dry eye in the room and I couldn't believe he was spilling his heart like that to everyone.

He continued, "Now you have the opportunity to build that life and career in the place you love. I hope that all your days are filled with happiness and the love that you show to others. And Kyle, that's my little sister, you better walk the line and treat her right."

We all laughed through our tears. Then Amy asked if she could share something. She is the quietest, sweetest person ever.

"I just wanted to say thank you to Pop and Sammy for pulling us all together again. I want the girls to know this happiness of our family and I want them to know the awesomeness of this place. Mac and I met here and we have never even been back to celebrate an anniversary and I want that to change. So thank you for reminding us of where and why we fell in love."

"Aww, I love you guys so much! This is the best Christmas ever!"

"And I will be your maid of honor!" Lizzy chimed in.

I had plenty of time to plan a wedding. I just wanted to soak in every minute of being engaged to Kyle Martin. I wanted to plan and dream of our future and make up for every minute I missed over the years. I wanted to date him and learn everything there was to know about him. I was engaged and I wanted to enjoy it.

Sitting on the couch, curled up beside Kyle, met all my expectations of a wonderful Christmas. The family all there and laughing and telling stories with each other was so worth more than any gift. I understood now why mom was the happiest when we were all together.

I had forgotten how much I missed being with these people. They were my people. They were the people that were most special to me in the entire world. I didn't tell them that, but I hoped they knew. I hoped they knew that they brought light into my darkest days and that just being with them lifted any load that I carried and reminded me of all the good things in my life that I take for granted each day.

The tree was flickering and the fire was cracking in the fire place. Dad was helping the girls with a puzzle. I thought about Mom and how much she would have loved this day, but I wasn't sad. I was happy because she had given us this gift of each other. She had spent her life making sure that we had memories to share with one another and our children. She gave up her dreams too, so that she could teach us about being a family. She used to tell me, "Lizzy, I know your brother and sister drive you crazy some days, but one day you will grow up and realize that these are the most important people in your life. These are the people that will always stand with you. You may fight with them, but they will always be there when you need them."

She was right again and I'm sure she was smiling big this Christmas day.

The End

ABOUT THE AUTHOR

Angela Lewis Buckner is a writer and artist. She loves the sea, her family and has a huge heart for dogs as you will discover in her writing.

Made in the USA
Columbia, SC
30 September 2020

21486807R00145